You can't

Cassie heard crackling on the line.

"Hello?"

More crackling. And then a sound like a gasp, a dry gust of wind.

"You can't run away."

The voice wasn't a whisper. It was a breeze. A burst of air.

A burst of foul air.

"You can't run away."

And then the line went dead. . . .

Other Point paperbacks
by R.L. Stine you will enjoy:

point

HIT and RUN

R.L. Stine

SCHOLASTIC INC.
New York Toronto London Auckland Sydney

No part of this publication may be reproduced in whole or in part, or stored in a retrieval system, or transmitted in any form or by any means, electronic, mechanical, photocopying, recording, or otherwise, without written permission of the publisher. For information regarding permission, write to Scholastic Inc., 730 Broadway, New York, NY 10003.

ISBN 0-590-45385-8

12 11   4 5 6 7/9

Printed in the U.S.A.   01

First Scholastic printing, June 1992

Contents

HIT and RUN

1

The Eyes Have It

Cassie Martin hung out with three boys.

Cassie had been athletic all her life, playing sports, swimming, bike-riding, and hanging out with the boys in her neighborhood. And when she got to high school, she didn't see any reason to change friends.

Short and thin, with crimped blonde hair, and lively green eyes in a face full of freckles, Cassie looked about twelve, even though she was nearly sixteen.

Cassie had a crush on one of the three boys she hung out with. Scott Baldwin. But it was a secret crush. Scott had no idea. To him, Cassie was just a pal.

Scott was one of those all-around guys who get their picture in about twenty places in the yearbook. Really good-looking in a teddy bear sort of way, Scott was a big, blond jock with brawny shoulders and a broad neck, but he also had brains.

He was starting fullback on the football team and an all-state wrestler. He was also class representative to the Student Government. He had an after-school job in his uncle's hardware store — and he managed to maintain a solid B-plus average.

Just about perfect. That's what Cassie thought.

But no one's perfect. Scott had his faults, she realized. For one thing, he had a really annoying laugh — a high-pitched giggle that made Cassie's teeth itch. For another, Scott was more of a follower than a leader.

Despite his big size, he was more of a sheep than a tiger.

Mainly, he was always ready to go along with the dumb jokes and schemes that Winks cooked up.

Bruce Winkleman was another one of the three guys Cassie hung out with. No one called him Bruce. Everyone called him Winks — except his mother.

Winks had stringy brown hair down to his shoulders, and he wore black-rimmed Buddy Holly glasses that were too big for his slender face. He had only one kind of smile — a devilish grin.

Winks was a good guy, too, after you got to know him. But what a joker. Sometimes Cassie wished he could be more serious. But then he wouldn't be Winks.

Cassie was at Scott's house on a Wednesday evening after dinner. They were supposed to study their government assignment. But Scott's parents had rushed out to go to an early movie, leaving Scott with the dinner dishes to wash, so Cassie helped him in the kitchen instead.

They had just about finished when Winks came marching in through the back door, as usual without knocking. He was carrying a cardboard box, a little smaller than a shoe box, which he set down on the kitchen counter.

It was a chilly winter night, about twenty-five or so outside, and windy, but Winks was wearing the same blue denim jacket he always wore, the one with his father's old war medals pinned up and down the front, and faded jeans with gaping holes at the knees.

He was wearing his devilish grin, too.

"I suppose you're wondering what's in the box," Winks said, pushing his heavy eyeglasses up on his short, pudgy nose.

"Not really," Cassie said, drying the last dinner plate and handing it to Scott to put away.

"You two look like you're married," Winks said.

Cassie tossed down the dish towel. She glanced at Scott, who looked embarrassed. "Yeah. We got married this morning," she told Winks. "But it's a secret. Our parents don't know yet."

Winks's devilish grin became more devilish. "When's the honeymoon?"

"What's in the box?" Scott asked, changing the subject. He took the dish towel and mopped up the countertop.

"Try to guess," Winks said, drumming his fingers on top of the box. "Is Eddie coming over?"

Eddie was the third guy, Cassie's other friend.

"I don't think so. Why?" Scott asked suspiciously.

"Aw, Winks." Cassie made a disgusted face, then lowered her eyes to the box. "Is this another dumb joke you're going to play on Eddie?"

Winks's dark eyes lit up behind his black-rimmed glasses. "It isn't dumb," he said. "It's . . . baad."

Scott let out his high-pitched giggle. He was always ready to play another joke on Eddie.

But Cassie worried that they'd played too many dumb jokes on their friend. Sure, Eddie was a good sport. In fact, he was *too* good a sport. If he'd get really mad once, Cassie thought, Winks and Scott would probably stop.

The only reason kids liked to play jokes on Eddie was because he was so quiet, and sort of timid and frightened-looking. His name was Eddie Katz, and some kids had started calling him Scaredy Katz.

He was short, about the same height as Cassie, and very wiry, with curly black hair. Eddie was one of those guys who blushed very easily. His cheeks always seemed to have dark red circles on them.

Eddie was smart and serious. He wanted to be a doctor, a difficult goal since his family was struggling financially and he'd have to make his own way through college and medical school.

"Call Eddie," Winks told Scott. "Get him over here."

"Okay. Sure." Scott reached for the red wall phone.

"What's in the box?" Cassie asked.

"Guess," Winks insisted.

"Your brain?"

Scott giggled and punched Eddie's number on the phone.

"Close," Winks said, grinning.

Scott got Eddie on the phone and told him to come over. Then he hung up. "He's coming. What's in the box?"

"It's an eyeball," Winks said, removing the lid and starting to lift the box to show them.

Cassie hid her eyes with her hand. "Don't show it to me. That's really gross!"

Scott stared at the box. "From an animal? What kind of animal?"

"From a human," Winks said. He replaced the lid.

"That's a human eye?" Scott asked. He giggled. "It's so *humongous!*"

"Gross," Cassie repeated. "Where'd you get it?"

"From an eye store," Winks cracked. "They were having a sale."

"I just ate," Scott said, holding his stomach.

"Winks — is that really a human eye?" Cassie asked, staring at the box.

He nodded, pleased with himself. "I got it from Eddie's cousin Jerry. He works at the city morgue. Downtown."

"Eddie's cousin gave you an eyeball?" Cassie asked, feeling sick.

"Yeah. He removed it from some corpse."

"Didn't the corpse need it for his funeral?" Cassie asked.

"I can't believe we're discussing this," Scott proclaimed, scratching his blond hair.

"He was being cremated, so he didn't need it," Winks informed them. He shook the box. The eyeball plopped against the sides.

"Yuck! Stop!" Cassie pleaded. "Really, Winks. I mean it."

"Did you ever get that new Polaroid you were talking about?" Winks asked Scott, giving the box one more good shake for Cassie's benefit.

"Yeah, I got it," Scott replied, straightening the sleeve of his blue-and-gold Avondale North High sweatshirt with the North High bulldog growling across the front.

"Well, go get it," Winks said. "I want a picture of Eddie's reaction when I do my eyeball trick."

"Your . . . eyeball trick?" Cassie asked reluctantly.

Winks flashed his evil grin at her. "You'll see."

Scott returned from his room carrying a yellow plastic camera. "All ready," he said.

"Is that a camera or a toy?" Winks asked sarcastically. "What *is* that — My First Camera?"

Cassie laughed. It did look like a baby camera.

"It's a really good camera," Scott insisted defensively. "You can take underwater pictures with it."

"Underwater Polaroids?" Cassie asked.

"Ooh — let's go try it out in the bathtub," Winks exclaimed.

"Don't look at me," Cassie cracked. "I'm not taking a bath with you, Winks."

Winks did an exaggerated pout. "Hold on to the camera, Scottso. And when I do my eyeball thing, get Eddie's face, okay?"

Scott nodded. He always agreed to everything Winks wanted.

"This is really gross," Cassie said, glancing at the box. "I can't believe Eddie's cousin gave that to you."

"He's a good guy," Winks said. "I guess he gets bored working at the morgue. He said business is really dead!"

Scott laughed. Cassie did, too, but she hated herself for it.

Such a bad joke.

A few minutes later, Eddie appeared at the kitchen door. He was wearing his blue down vest over a bulky black-and-red sweater, and a blue wool ski cap. "It's cold," he said, stepping into the kitchen, his cheeks bright red.

"How's it going?" Scott asked.

Cassie looked around. Winks had disappeared from the room.

"Okay, I guess," Eddie said, pulling off the ski cap and straightening his black, curly hair with his hand. He smiled at Cassie. "Hi."

She returned his greeting, lowering her eyes guiltily to the yellow camera beside Scott on the kitchen counter. She had a momentary urge to warn Eddie that Winks was about to play a trick on him.

But it was only momentary.

"Were you doing homework?" she asked Eddie.

He shook his head. "No. I was studying for my driver's test. You know. That booklet they give you for the written exam."

"When do you take it?" Scott asked, his eyes on the doorway behind Eddie.

"In a few weeks," Eddie replied, tossing his vest onto a tall kitchen stool. "It looks pretty easy. It's all multiple choice."

"I took it last week," Cassie said. "I only missed one question. The one about U-turns. I couldn't remember if they were legal or not."

"So you got your temporary? When do you take the driver's test?" Eddie asked.

"In a few days," Cassie replied excitedly.

At that moment, Winks entered from the hallway, holding both hands over his right eye, his head bowed.

"Hey — Winks," Eddie greeted him.

His hands cupped over his eye, Winks groaned.

Here it comes, Cassie told herself, holding her breath.

"What's wrong with your eye?" Scott asked, helping the joke along.

"I don't know," Winks said, stepping up close to

Eddie. "I — I think I got something in it. There! I got it out!"

Keeping his eye tightly closed, Winks lowered his hand, revealing the big, wet eyeball in his palm.

Winks screamed.

Eddie's mouth dropped open. His cheeks blazed. His entire face burned scarlet.

Scott flashed the camera.

Cassie laughed.

But she stopped laughing when Eddie's eyes rolled up into his head and, uttering a low moan, he slumped backward onto the linoleum.

His head hit the floor with a solid *thud*.

Scott flashed the camera again.

"I don't believe it!" Winks cried gleefully, staring down at Eddie's unmoving form. "He fainted! Scott — photo op! Photo op!"

Scott flashed another photo.

"Wait! Stop!" Cassie cried, bending over Eddie. "Eddie, are you okay?"

Eddie didn't move.

She grabbed his wrist. Slapped his face. Felt his red cheek. Shook his head.

"Hey — " The grin faded from Winks's face. He was still holding the eyeball.

"Winks, I — I don't think he's breathing," Cassie cried. She held Eddie's limp hand. "I — I think he's dead!"

2
A Driving Lesson

Cassie let go of the hand, and it fell limply to the floor.

Scott uttered a choking sound. He backed up against the counter, his hands shoved into his jeans pockets.

"Come on," Winks said quietly, staring at Cassie, then moving his eyes down to Eddie's still form.

Eddie's eyes were closed. One leg was twisted at an odd angle under his body.

Winks set the eyeball down on the counter and wiped his hand off on a dish towel. "Come on," he repeated. "It was just a joke."

Pushing his glasses up on his nose, he crossed the kitchen and bent down over Eddie. "Just a joke," he repeated.

Eddie groaned and sat up. "What happened?" he asked, raising a hand to his forehead. "Did I black out?"

The other three all whooped for joy.

"You're okay!" Cassie cried happily.

Eddie lay back down on the linoleum. "I'm not so sure," he said weakly. "My head . . ."

"You hit it when you fell," Cassie told him.

"Do you believe it? He fainted!" Winks cried, shaking his head. "What a man! What a man!"

"Give him a break," Scott said.

"What's the matter, Eddie — didn't you ever see an eyeball before?" Winks asked. He turned to Scott. "I expected a good reaction — but not *that* good!" He and Scott laughed.

"Wish I'd gotten a photo of *Winks's* face when he thought Eddie was dead!" Scott exclaimed.

"Very funny," Winks said sarcastically. "At least I didn't faint like an old lady!" He scooped up the eyeball, which had yellowed quite a bit and appeared to be oozing some kind of clear liquid, and dropped it into the box.

Eddie pulled himself to his feet, still looking pale. "That is really gross," he said to Winks. "Where'd you get it?"

"I made it in shop," Winks cracked. "No. It was on my lunch tray."

"Actually, there were two of them," said Cassie, "but Winks ate one."

"Ohh, gross," Scott groaned and pretended to throw up in the sink.

Eddie reached for his down vest and ski cap. "Well, thanks for the entertainment, guys. Guess I'll get home."

"Hey, you're feeling better? Let's do something," Winks suggested, holding him back.

"I've got a lot of homework," Eddie said, his cheeks reddening.

"So do we," said Scott and Cassie in unison.

"They're married," Winks explained to Eddie.

"Huh?" Eddie scratched his black hair, then pulled the wool ski cap down over his forehead.

"We can do homework any time," Winks said. "Let's do something more worthwhile."

"Like play with an eyeball?" Cassie snapped. She shuddered, thinking about the hideous thing.

"Let's . . . practice our driving," Winks suggested.

"We can't!" Cassie cried.

"Drive what?" Scott asked.

"Your parents' Volvo," Winks said. "It's in the garage. I saw it when I came up."

Scott's parents had two cars. Cassie realized they must have taken the Toyota to the movie.

"We can't," Cassie said again. "None of us has a license. We aren't allowed to drive by ourselves."

"You have a temporary," Winks said. "That's almost a license."

"You have a temporary brain," Cassie cracked.

"I don't think it's a good idea to take my parents' car," Scott said, fiddling with his sweatshirt sleeve. "No. No way. If they found out, they'd *kill* me!"

Fifteen minutes later they were in their coats, rolling up the garage door.

Scott just can't say no to Winks, Cassie thought. We shouldn't be doing this. What if Scott's parents find out? What if the police stop us for some reason, and discover that none of us has a license?

What if we're in an accident?

She had to admit it was kind of exciting, too.

Bad Kids Out for a Thrill Ride.

She was always making up headlines in her mind. She liked the sound of that one.

"Hey, the car is scratched," Winks said, running his hand along a deep scratch in the driver's door. "You do this, Scott?"

"No way," Scott said quickly. "I haven't had a chance to put any scratches on it yet."

"Who's going to drive first? Eddie?" Winks asked, shoving Eddie toward the driver's door.

"Hey — no way!" Eddie backed out of the garage.

"Come on, Eddie," Winks urged. "We'll just drive to the mall. You know. The parking lot behind the stores. It's always empty at night. We can practice parking."

"No way," Eddie insisted. "You drive, Winks. It's your idea."

"I'll take a turn," Winks said, glancing at Cassie, who was already climbing into the back seat of the silver Volvo. "Okay, Scott, you go first. It's your car."

"Fine," Scott agreed quickly. "I've driven this car before. With my dad, I mean. This is the car

I've been practicing in." He slid behind the wheel. "Ooh — it's cold in here."

All four of them were settled now, their breath steaming up to the ceiling. Eddie sat beside Scott in the front, who was struggling to get his shoulder seat belt to click in.

"Peel out," Winks said enthusiastically.

"I can't believe I agreed to this," Eddie said, tugging off the ski hat and tossing it onto the dashboard in front of him.

"We're just practicing," Winks insisted.

Scott stared at the gearshift. "What does 'R' stand for? 'Right This Way'?"

Cassie and Winks laughed. Eddie's face contracted with worry. He stared straight ahead, eyes up as if praying, as Scott backed out of the garage and down the driveway.

"If we get caught, we'll *never* get our licenses," Eddie whined, sitting stiffly, alertly in his seat.

"We won't get caught," Cassie assured him, leaning over the front seat to pat Eddie's shoulder.

"If the cops come after us, we'll just outrace them," Winks said. "Let's see what this thing can do, Scottso."

"Hey — not funny!" Eddie cried, turning back to glare at Winks.

"Don't worry," Cassie said. "Scott's a good driver, Eddie. He's very careful. I've driven with him when we were with his family."

"She's right," Scott said seriously, making a

sharp right turn onto Market Avenue. And, then, suddenly, he lifted both hands high in the air. "Look, Ma — no hands!"

Cassie laughed. Scott can be so cute sometimes, she thought. Like a big, funny teddy bear.

Eddie, she saw, was not amused by any of this. The poor guy was really frightened, she realized.

"Hey, Winks — what'd you do with the eye?" Scott asked, slowing for a red light.

"The eye?" The evil grin returned to Winks's face. "Well, I put it somewhere."

"Somewhere? Where's somewhere?" Scott demanded.

"In your refrigerator," Winks said, grinning at Cassie. "You know. For when your dad comes into the kitchen for his midnight snack. He opens the refrigerator, pulls out the box, licking his chops, and — bingo!"

Everyone laughed.

"Watch out for that truck," Eddie warned, pointing.

"Eddie, that truck is two lanes away!" Scott cried.

"Well, I didn't know if you saw it," Eddie said, adjusting his seat belt.

When they got to the Avondale Mall, it looked pretty crowded, so they kept on driving. Following the old Route 12, they soon found themselves outside of town, in flat farm country, the road smooth and unswerving.

The new expressway had been open for less than a year, but it had already taken almost all of the traffic that had previously traveled on Route 12.

"The road is all ours," Scott said, pulling the silver Volvo over onto the grassy shoulder. "Someone else's turn. Eddie?"

Eddie shook his head. "Not me."

Cassie leaned forward. "You want to pass your test, don't you?" she asked. "This is a perfect place to practice. It's totally straight, and there isn't another car in sight."

"Well, I *do* want to pass," Eddie said thoughtfully.

Scott opened his door, letting in a blast of cold air. The air this far out of town smelled fresh and sweet. Cassie inhaled deeply, smiling.

"Come on, man," Scott urged.

Eddie disengaged his seat belt and stepped out of the car to trade places with Scott.

"I don't believe he's doing it," Winks whispered to Cassie. "Eddie's always such a wimp. But he's got more guts than I thought."

"He's very competitive," Cassie said. "He likes to pass tests."

Eddie slammed the door. The roof light went out. The darkness seemed to close in on them. He was shorter than Scott, so he moved the seat up.

An oil truck roared by, the driver honking as he passed.

"Hey — someone else is on this road!" Winks exclaimed.

"Ease it out slowly," Scott instructed Eddie, turning in the passenger seat to face him. "You don't have to press hard on the gas. The car has lots of power."

Eddie put both hands at the top of the steering wheel and pulled the car off the shoulder and onto the narrow highway.

"That's it. Very good," Scott assured him.

"I'm pretty comfortable with my dad's car," Eddie said, his eyes straight ahead on the twin beams of light from the headlights. "But it's an old Chevy Nova, the kind they don't make anymore. It takes a while to adjust to a newer car."

"You're doing fine," Scott said, glancing back at Cassie.

"Better slow down," Winks urged. "You're already going fifteen!" He laughed.

"I thought I was going faster," Eddie said, sounding nervous, his hands together on top of the wheel.

"You'd better speed up a little," Scott urged.

"Drive at whatever speed is comfortable for you," Cassie said. "There's no one around, so it doesn't matter."

"But you won't pass your test if you go this slow out on the open road," Winks said.

Eddie immediately sped up.

They passed a sprawling farmhouse, all of its

windows bathed in orange light. Log fences rolled by, dark shadows against a darker ground.

A short while later, they drove under the Hanson Underpass, a low stone bridge that had been built over the highway at least a hundred years before.

"I'm starting to feel like I'm in control," Eddie said. He pressed down a little harder on the gas pedal, and the car sped up.

"EDDIE! LOOK OUT!" Winks screamed.

Eddie slammed down on the brake.

"No! Oh, no!" Cassie cried.

The tires squealed in protest, and the car hurtled into a desperate spin.

3

No Brakes

The car spun wildly over the road, then came to a jolting stop on the soft, grassy shoulder.

Cassie lurched forward into the back of the driver's seat. Eddie uttered a small cry as his chest hit the steering wheel. His eyes searched the darkness beyond the windshield.

There was nothing there.

No car or truck in sight.

"April fool," Winks said quietly.

Scott started to laugh.

"Gotcha," Winks said, reaching forward to pat Eddie on the shoulder.

Eddie jerked his shoulder away and spun around, the fear on his face giving way to anger. "Winks — " He was too angry to talk.

Cassie found herself laughing, more out of relief than amusement. "Winks, you could've gotten us

killed," she said, giving him a hard shove that sent
him sprawling against the door.

"Anything for a laugh," Winks replied. "Ow.
That hurt." He rubbed his shoulder.

She shoved him again.

Scott had tears in his eyes from laughing so hard.
"I believed you, Winks," he said. "I believed you,
man. You're such a good actor. You sounded so
panicked."

Scowling, Eddie shoved the gearshift into park,
pushed open the car door, and climbed out. "See
you guys," he muttered bitterly.

"Hey, Eddie — wait!" Cassie called.

But he started to walk off quickly into the
darkness.

"Eddie — come back!" Scott jumped out of the
car and went running after him. Cassie and Winks
followed behind, leaving their car doors open, dim
yellow light seeping out in a small circle, the hum
of the engine the only sound except for the crunch
of their sneakers on the cold ground.

Scott caught up with Eddie, who kept walking,
his breath rising up in gray puffs against the starless
black sky. "Wait up, man." Eddie didn't stop.

Scott grabbed the shoulder of his down vest. "It
was just a joke, Eddie."

Eddie spun around angrily, quickly raising both
arms to break Scott's grip. "Everything isn't a
joke," he said angrily. "Some things shouldn't be
joked about."

"There was no one around. I knew we wouldn't get hurt," Winks said, breathing hard, ducking his head down into his jacket as he caught up with Eddie and Scott.

Eddie shoved his hands into his jeans pockets and glared at him. "It wasn't funny, Winks," he said softly. He turned and started walking along the road.

"Eddie — come back!" Cassie called. "Come on. It's cold out here."

The three of them hurried after him. Cassie glanced back at the car, a shadow inside a dim circle of light, far behind them.

"I'm sorry," Winks called. "Eddie, I'm sorry. Okay? It was a stupid joke. I'm sorry."

"We've got to get back," Scott said, trying to read his watch in the darkness. "I've got to get the car back in the garage before my parents get home."

"Come on, Eddie," Cassie urged.

Finally, Eddie stopped. He turned to face them, his hands still shoved in his pockets. Cassie saw that he was shivering. From anger? she wondered. Or from the cold?

"Okay. Let's go back," Eddie said quietly, and started walking toward the car, lowering his head against the wind.

They were all cold by the time they got back to the car. Scott climbed behind the wheel and turned the heater up to high. Eddie climbed in back beside Cassie.

"Hey — it's my turn to drive," Winks protested, buckling the shoulder seat belt.

"No way," Scott said, easing the car onto the road. "Driving practice is over for tonight."

"I didn't get a turn, either," Cassie complained.

"Winks took up all our time with his dumb joke," Scott said. And then he glanced at the glowing yellow clock in the center of the dashboard. "Oh, no! Look how late it is! I'm going to be dead meat. Dead meat!"

He jammed his foot down on the accelerator, and the car responded with a roar.

"Whoa!" Winks cried, sliding down in his seat.

"I've got to get home!" Scott said as the car picked up speed.

Cassie leaned forward and glanced at the speedometer. "Scott — you're going eighty!"

"I can't help it," he replied, staring straight ahead into the twin cones of white light from the headlights. "If they get home before I do . . ." He didn't finish his thought.

He didn't have to. They all knew what kind of trouble he'd be in. What kind of trouble they'd *all* be in.

They roared under the Hanson Underpass. A few seconds later, the brightly lit farmhouse slid by, this time on the other side of the car. The low, flat fields gave way to woods, then clusters of houses.

"Slow down," Cassie urged. "We're back in town."

Eddie, she realized, had been silent ever since they'd returned to the car. She glanced over at him. He was staring out his window, his face expressionless, the wool ski cap pulled protectively low over his forehead.

A traffic light appeared up ahead. It blinked from yellow to red. Scott sped right through it.

"Scott — slow down!" Cassie yelled.

"I'm — I'm trying!" Scott cried, gripping the wheel tightly with both hands.

"Huh? What do you mean?"

Scott pumped the brake pedal hard several times. "The brakes — they're out!" he exclaimed.

The car roared through another intersection.

"No brakes!" Scott cried, his eyes wide with horror.

4
De-Pantsed

"Lame, Scott. Real lame," Winks said, shaking his head.

"But the brakes — " Scott insisted as the big Volvo roared past the Avondale Mall.

"No one is buying it," Winks said, turning to look back at Cassie and Eddie. "You're just not convincing. You're a bad actor."

Scott slowed the car down. His excited face drooped into a disappointed pout. "How about you, Eddie? You believed me, didn't you?"

Eddie stared silently out the window.

"Eddie isn't talking," Cassie told Scott. "Winks is right. That was lame."

Scott giggled and turned sharply onto Market Avenue.

"Some have it. Some don't," Winks said.

"What did I do wrong?" Scott asked seriously. "I even made it look like I was pumping the brakes."

"But you didn't sound scared enough," Winks told him. "It sounded like a put-on."

"I'll bet Eddie bought it," Scott said.

Eddie didn't reply.

A few minutes later, Scott pulled the car up the driveway and into the garage. "My parents aren't back," he said, very relieved.

The four of them piled out of the car. "Nice drive," Cassie said, stretching.

"Yeah. Thanks for the driving lesson, guys," Eddie said sarcastically.

"Hey — it can talk!" Winks said, and slapped Eddie on the shoulder.

"It was kind of fun," Cassie admitted, "in a crazy kind of way."

"I've got to get home," Eddie said.

"I'll drive you!" Winks joked.

Eddie didn't smile. "See you." He jogged down the driveway to the street.

Cassie stared up at the sky, searching for the moon, but could see only shades of gray against gray. She shivered, suddenly chilled. "Guess I'd better get home, too."

"I think Eddie was really freaked," Winks said.

Cassie and Scott quickly agreed. "Yeah, he was freaked," Cassie said.

Winks's face lit up with a truly evil grin.

"Scott, how can you pay forty dollars more for sneakers just because you can pump them up?" Cassie stared down disapprovingly at the gleaming new white sneakers on Scott's feet.

"They feel good," Scott replied. "Real bouncy." He jumped straight up in the air and pretended to shoot a basketball lay-up.

A woman and her two children had to scramble out of his way. "You're blocking the door," she said, flashing him an annoyed look as she ushered her kids away.

"I can jump about three feet," Scott said, looking very pleased.

"Oh, that'll come in real handy during a wrestling match," Cassie cracked. "You just bought those sneakers because everyone else is."

Scott was such a great guy, she kept thinking. If only he weren't such a sheep.

"They're cool," Scott said, admiring his sneakers as he followed her out of the store and into the crowded mall. "They're way cool."

It was Saturday afternoon, and Cassie didn't know what she was doing here with him. There were a hundred more constructive things she could be doing than following Scott around the Avondale Mall, watching him buy ridiculously expensive sneakers.

"Hey — look. A two-for-one sale on sweat-pants," Scott said, pointing to a sign in a window across the wide aisle.

"Ooh. Thrills," Cassie said sarcastically.

He stared at her, surprised. "What's your problem?"

She shrugged. "No problem."

"Well, let's check out the sweatpants, okay?"

"Yeah. Maybe they have ones that inflate," Cassie joked.

"Ha-ha," he said, making a face.

"I'll meet you over there," Cassie said, pointing to a record store. "There's a CD I want to buy."

"Which one?" Scott asked.

Before she could answer, Winks appeared. He was wearing a bright yellow sweater and green corduroys. "How's my favorite married couple?" he asked, leering first at Cassie, then at Scott. "Buying socks together?"

Cassie rolled her eyes. Scott punched Winks playfully on the shoulder. "Where'd you get that sweater, Winks? You lose a contest or something?"

"What's wrong with this sweater?" Winks asked, fingering a sleeve.

"It's a little yellow, isn't it?" Cassie asked.

"A little."

"You look like an Easter chick," Scott told him.

"Happy Easter," Winks said, smoothing the sweater front with one hand. "You hear what happened to Eddie in school yesterday?"

"No. What?" Cassie asked, waving across the aisle to some girls she recognized from Avondale North.

"Someone de-pantsed him," Winks said, grinning.

"Huh?"

"Well, not exactly," Winks said, following Cassie's glance at the girls across the aisle. "Actually, some kid took Eddie's pants from his gym locker. You know, while he was in gym. And he had to go to class the rest of the day in his smelly gym shorts." Winks laughed. "You should've seen Eddie's face. It was as red as a tomato the whole day."

"I can just picture it," Scott said, grinning. He scratched his head. "Poor Eddie."

"Eddie's such a nice guy," Cassie said. "Why is everyone always picking on him?"

"Because he's so easy," Winks replied, pushing his black-rimmed glasses up on his nose. "Remember Wednesday night? I'll bet *anything* Eddie believed that Scott had no brakes. That was so lame, but I just know Eddie believed it."

"So he's a little gullible," Cassie said. "That doesn't explain why everybody has to pick on him all the time."

"There's one kid like that in every class," Winks said. "One kid everyone likes to pound on. Eddie just happens to be that kid. He's used to it."

"You think so?" Cassie asked.

"Yeah, sure," was Winks's reply. He glanced down at the floor. "Hey, Scott — don't tell me. You bought sneakers you can pump up?"

"Yeah. They feel good," Scott said, bouncing up and down in them.

"I knew a guy who couldn't deflate his once he had them on," Winks said. "He had to get the fire department to chop them off."

"Who did it to Eddie?" Cassie asked, interrupting the sneaker conversation.

"What?" Winks was still staring down at the shiny, white sneakers.

"Who took Eddie's pants from his gym locker?" Cassie demanded.

"I did. Of course," Winks said, grinning proudly.

Cassie and Scott took the North Avondale bus from the mall to her house. Actually, it let them off two blocks from her house. And as they walked, the heavy, gray clouds that had darkened the sky all day parted, allowing some reluctant rays of sunshine to poke through.

Cassie unzipped her coat. The air was still cold, but the sun felt good on her face. It had been a long winter — cold, but with little snow.

When Scott stopped at the hedges in front of her house, put his hands on her shoulders, and kissed her, it came as a real surprise.

The kiss was awkward. He missed her lips and got her chin. His face felt cold against hers.

He stepped back, letting his hands drop from her shoulders, staring at her as if waiting to judge her reaction.

Cassie didn't know how to react.

She'd had a secret crush on Scott for months. But she'd had no idea he saw her as anything else except the friend he had grown up a block away from.

"Winks keeps saying we're married," Scott said, blushing, a strange smile on his handsome face.

Cassie laughed. "Then we can do better than that," she said impulsively. And she grabbed the back of Scott's neck, pulled his face down to hers, and kissed him, their lips on target this time.

When it ended and they smiled awkwardly at each other, Cassie felt strangely unsettled.

Maybe this is wrong, she thought. Maybe I'm messing up a good friendship here.

He reached for her again, but she pulled back. "See you later," she said breathlessly and turned and ran up the drive, leaving him standing there, his expression disappointed, almost sad.

That night, the four of them gathered at Eddie's house after dinner. The small house was hot, almost steamy, and smelled of meat loaf.

Huddled in the narrow living room, two on the couch, two on the threadbare carpet, they were discussing what to do.

"We could go to a movie," Scott said.

"There's nothing good playing," Cassie told him. "I checked."

"There's a dance at the school," Scott suggested. "I think they're having a DJ and a live band. You know, the band that plays at that dance club on the south side. What are they called?"

"You mean RapManiacs?" Eddie asked, small circles of red forming on his cheeks.

"Yeah."

"They're putrid," Eddie said. "They really rot."

"Might be a hoot," Winks said thoughtfully.

"No way," Cassie said. "I'd rather read my government text."

Eddie got up from the couch and walked to the picture window in the center of the room. He stared out into a clear, cool night. "We could go for a drive," he said, his back to them.

The other three reacted in shock.

"You want to go for another drive? After Wednesday night?" Cassie asked. She walked over to Eddie and felt his forehead. "No. No temperature."

Eddie laughed. "We could all use some real driving practice," he said. "You know. No fooling around."

"My parents are home," Scott said. "I can't get the car."

"Our car is here," Eddie said, pointing down to the curb. "My parents are at a party two blocks away. They won't be home till really late. We could take it."

"Great!" Scott exclaimed, climbing to his feet.

Eddie turned to Winks. "But you've got to promise no jokes."

Winks put on his innocent face. "Who, me?"

"We won't need headlights," Cassie cracked. "Winks can run ahead of us in that sweater!"

Everyone laughed but Winks. He yanked at the bright yellow wool. "My grandmother bought me this sweater!"

"Your grandmother is color blind," Eddie said.

"How'd you know?" Winks replied.

"Well, how about it?" Eddie demanded, staring at Winks.

"Okay, okay. No jokes," Winks agreed. "As long as I get a long turn."

"We'll all get turns," Eddie said, hurrying to the coat closet by the front door. He tossed Cassie's down coat across the room to her. "We're all taking the driver's test in the next couple of weeks, right? So we need all the practice we can get."

"Where should we drive?" Cassie asked. "There's so much traffic in town on Saturday nights. Someone might recognize us."

"Let's go back on Route 12," Scott suggested. "It's so deserted. And so straight. It's great for practicing."

"Okay," Eddie agreed, pulling the blue ski cap over his dark, curly hair. "Let's do it."

The four of them stepped out of the house and headed down the drive, their sneakers crunching over unraked, dead leaves. The air was cool and crisp. Someone a few houses down had a fire going in their chimney, sending a tangy, pine aroma wafting over the neighborhood.

Cassie took a deep breath. Such a great smell. "So why'd you change your mind?" she asked Eddie as they walked. "I mean, after Wednesday — "

"I was a jerk on Wednesday night," Eddie said, avoiding her glance. "I acted like a baby. So I thought I'd make up for it. And . . ."

"And?"

"I really want to pass the driver's test. I really want to practice so I can get my license," he said, raising his eyes to hers.

Cassie felt a chill as she climbed into the back seat.

This is kind of dangerous, she thought. None of us has a license. If something goes wrong . . . if we're caught . . .

She shook her head hard as if chasing those thoughts from her mind, and slammed the car door shut.

Nothing was going to go wrong, she decided.

Nothing.

5

A Bump in the Road

The streets in town were clogged with cars. Saturday night. Date night. Market Avenue was jammed with high school kids cruising back and forth along the strip at ten miles an hour.

"In a few weeks, I'll be cruising Market, too," Eddie said cheerfully. He slowed for a light, hit the brake too hard, and the tires squealed as the car jerked to a stop.

"Smooth it out," Winks advised him from beside Cassie in the back seat.

"Thanks for the good advice," Eddie said sarcastically, his eyes raised to the traffic light.

"My turn next," Cassie said.

"What *is* this car — some kind of antique?" Scott asked from the front passenger seat, his eyes surveying the dashboard.

"No, it only smells like an antique," Winks cracked.

"It's a Nova," Eddie said, drumming his fingers impatiently on the steering wheel. "An old Chevy. My dad bought it third-hand for two hundred dollars."

"He got ripped off," Winks said.

A horn honked impatiently behind them.

"Eddie, the light's green," Winks said. "Green means go."

Eddie stepped on the gas, and the car lurched forward, sputtering a little as it shifted. "You're full of good advice tonight, Winks," Eddie said good-naturedly.

Traffic thinned out past the mall. Eddie made the turn onto Route 12, glancing in the rearview mirror as if checking to make sure he wasn't being followed.

"No one's on your tail. You're driving like a pro," Winks said.

"I thought I saw a cop behind us," Eddie said, picking up speed on the nearly deserted highway.

"Don't get paranoid," Scott warned, giggling.

"When do I get my turn?" Cassie asked impatiently.

Eddie obediently pulled the car over to the side of the road. A pickup truck with only one headlight rumbled past. Cassie got out of the car and traded places with him.

"Move the seat up if you have to," Eddie instructed.

"No. We're about the same height," Cassie said, studying the dashboard.

"Both shrimps," Winks cracked.

Cassie ignored him. "Okay. Fasten your seat belts. Here we go!" she announced and, pushing down hard on the gas pedal, pulled the car back onto the old highway, the tires whirring, spitting gravel, and then settling onto the road.

Cassie drove smoothly. After nearly half an hour, cruising through several small farm towns, past dark, flat fields that seemed to stretch on forever, she turned the wheel over to Winks.

He kept his promise to Eddie, driving seriously and carefully. In typical fashion, he kept up a running commentary on every move he made — "I'm looking in the mirror now . . . and now I'm sliding my hand down the wheel. . . . I'm scratching my ear with one hand . . . and now I'm checking the speedometer . . . picking my nose now. . . . " — until the other three begged him to shut up.

Finally, he relinquished the driver's seat to Scott, who drove without incident along the nearly empty highway, taking them most of the way back toward Avondale.

"Hey, we're all going to be pros by the time we take the driver's test," Winks exclaimed happily. "I could drive this car with my eyes closed."

"I heard the parallel-parking test is real easy," Scott said, pulling over to the shoulder so that Eddie could drive the rest of the way home.

"If you take the test in a really small car, you can't flunk it," Cassie said, staring out the window at a tall silo, dark against the purple sky. "They give you this much room." She gestured with her hands. "Enough room to park a moving van in."

"That's what I'm taking the test in," Winks said. "A moving van. You know. More of a challenge that way."

"Remind me to laugh later," Cassie replied.

For the ride home, Eddie climbed behind the wheel. Cassie remained in the passenger seat next to him. The other two boys slumped in the back, their knees on the seatbacks in front of them.

"After I get my license, I'd love to get a jeep," Eddie said, glancing in the rearview mirror, then at Cassie. "Maybe a Renegade. Or a Cherokee."

"Those are way cool," Scott agreed from the back seat.

They were approaching the Hanson Underpass. The low, stone bridge loomed gray-green in the yellow headlights.

Cassie yawned. The warm air from the heater was making her sleepy.

But she snapped wide awake when the man suddenly came into view in the middle of the road.

The headlights caught his startled expression. He stood staring at them, frozen, his arms at his sides.

Eddie cried out and slammed his foot on the brake.

The tires squealed as the car began to slide.

To Cassie, her mouth open wide in a silent

scream, it all seemed to happen in slow motion.

She saw that the man was wearing a tie and jacket. And a baseball cap.

She saw his wide-eyed stare. The expression of horror on his face, so bright, so unearthly bright in the glare of the headlights.

Then he appeared to be standing right in the windshield.

Then she felt the bump.

The surprisingly quiet *thud* of impact.

The man's expression didn't change.

His body flew straight up in the air.

The tires squealed again.

Closing her eyes, Cassie continued to scream, but no sound came out.

She felt another bump as the front tires rolled over the man.

And then the car finally came to a stop.

6
Hit and Run

When Cassie was a little girl of seven or eight, her parents gave her a white fluffball of a kitten. She named the kitten Fluffy, and it became her constant companion, immediately taking the place of all her stuffed animals.

She treated the kitten like a stuffed animal, carrying it in her arms everywhere she went, even sleeping with it cuddled under her chin.

"She's so attached to it," she heard her mother telling a friend over the phone.

Attached to it. The phrase stuck in her mind.

When her mother warned her not to take Fluffy into the front yard, Cassie ignored her. She was *attached* to Fluffy, after all.

Besides, it was a pretty spring day, the sun warm, the air soft and fragrant. Fluffy shouldn't be cooped up in the house, little blonde Cassie decided. Fluffy should come outside and play with her.

Out in the sunshine, with the apple trees blos-

soming pink and white all down the block, Fluffy
didn't want to stay in Cassie's arms. The kitten
wanted to explore.

And run.

And when Fluffy ran into the street, ignoring the
little girl's frantic cries, Cassie felt a terror inside
her that she had never experienced.

A cold, paralyzing terror.

The sound of the squealing red car. The sight of
the black tire track over Fluffy's flattened white
fur.

And then the tears.

The tears that wouldn't stop. The tears she didn't
want to stop.

Cassie saw it and heard it again and again. When-
ever she closed her eyes. Awake or in dreams.

The squeal. The black tire track.

The feeling of terror.

The same feeling she was experiencing now as
she and the three boys climbed silently out of the
old Chevy. The same paralyzing, cold-all-over terror that made her feel as if she weighed a thousand
pounds, as if she were a block of ice about to
crumble.

They were directly under the Hanson Overpass.
The car headlights bounced off the old stones. Someone had spray-painted a name in huge orange letters
on one side: MARGO '90.

Silence. The air was still. Not a sound except for
their breathing.

"Mister — are you okay?" Eddie was the first to break the silence. "Can you talk?"

The man, on his back in front of the car, stared lifelessly up at them as they huddled over him. Cold, gray eyes. His blue-and-red Chicago Cubs cap had somehow stayed on his head. His navy-blue necktie was lying straight up over his shoulder, the collar of his white shirt unbuttoned.

"Mister — ?"

Cassie wanted to bend over the man, to grab his hand, to say something to him. But she stood there, behind Scott, trembling now, trembling all over, her hands raised to her face.

Standing in front of the twin beams of light, the light bouncing back at them off the old stone bridge, it all seemed so bright. Not daylight bright. But eerily bright, as if they were in a horror movie, an unnatural world where you were forced to see everything you didn't want to see so clearly, so brightly.

Eddie was the first to overcome his fear enough to bend down and grab the man's wrist.

He dropped it immediately.

"He's dead." Eddie mouthed the words.

"He can't be!" Winks cried, standing timidly by the side of the car, behind the others.

"He's dead," Eddie said a little louder. "Look at his eyes."

They looked at the dull gray eyes staring up at the sky, unblinking.

I'll never forget those horrid eyes, Cassie thought.

She pictured the black tire tracks on her white kitten.

I'll never forget those eyes.

Scott put a hand on her shoulder. "Yeah. He's dead," he said, his voice a whisper. He squeezed Cassie's shoulder. "What are we going to do?"

"I — I *killed* him!" Eddie cried, a loud shriek of horror that startled them all. Eddie dropped to his knees on the pavement and buried his face in his hands.

"Eddie — " Cassie started. But the words didn't come. She leaned back against Scott.

"I killed him!" Eddie cried again.

Cassie gulped a deep breath of cool air and pulled away from Scott's grip. She dropped down beside Eddie, surprised at how cold the pavement felt through the knees of her jeans.

"Eddie, stop — "

He dropped his hands to his side and gazed at her, his face swollen and red in the yellow light from the headlights, his dark eyes wet with tears. "Cassie — I ran over him."

"It was an accident," she said softly.

She wanted to hug Eddie, to comfort him somehow. But she couldn't raise her arms, couldn't move. She turned away for a brief second and stared again at the corpse's wide eyes beneath the Cubs cap.

"But he's dead," Eddie wailed. "What are we going to do?"

Cassie raised her eyes and saw Winks walking toward them, a determined look on his face. "Winks — " she called to him. But he ignored her and, with a loud groan, hunkered over the body.

"Winks, what are you doing?" Scott, his face hidden in shadows, called.

Winks grabbed the dead man's waist and pushed him onto his side. Then he reached into his back pocket and pulled out a flat, brown wallet.

"Winks!" Cassie cried, horrified.

Was Winks going to rob a corpse?

"I just want to see who he is," Winks said. Holding the wallet open with both hands, he held it in front of a headlight.

"What is he *doing*?" Eddie asked Cassie, shaking his head, his face twisted in fright and panic.

"Brandt Tinkers," Winks announced. "His name is Brandt Tinkers."

"Is — is there an address?" Scott asked, still hidden in shadows, his voice shrill and high-pitched.

"Why do we need an address?" Eddie exploded. "Are we going to drop him off at his house? He's dead! Don't you understand? I *killed* him!"

Cassie finally managed to reach out and put her hands on Eddie's shoulders. "Be calm," she whispered, even though her heart was thudding like a bass drum in her chest. "Be calm, Eddie. It was an accident. An accident."

Winks returned the wallet to the dead man's back pocket, then made a sour face. "I feel sick. I really do." He gagged, raised his hand over his mouth, his eyes going wide behind the dark-framed glasses, and ran behind the car to vomit.

"When my parents find out I took the car, they'll *kill* me!" Eddie wailed. "How could this happen? How?"

Cassie held on to him tightly, but couldn't find any comforting words. She found herself thinking about what *her* parents would say. They'll never trust me again, she realized. They'll always be suspicious of me, of where I'm going, what I'm doing.

She turned to look down the dark highway. No one coming. No lights. Nothing moving.

"We've got to get out of here," Winks said, reappearing by the driver's side of the car, leaning against the door. "I just puked my guts out."

"What do you mean — get out of here?" Eddie asked, jumping unsteadily to his feet. He looked very confused.

"We can't stay here," Winks said impatiently, pulling open the car door. "We have to go. We *have* to!"

Cassie climbed to her feet, feeling as if she weighed a ton. She stared down at the corpse. "Winks — "

"I know what you're going to say," Winks replied heatedly, speaking rapidly, still leaning against the car. "But we can't do anything for this guy now.

He's dead. We can't get an ambulance for him. We can't help him. It's too late. So we have to help ourselves."

"He's right," Scott said, stepping into the light, his hands jammed into his jacket pockets. "We don't have driver's licenses. The police will fry our butts. Our lives will be ruined. Everyone will know what we did. We could even go to jail or something."

"But we can't just take off," Cassie said, glancing at Eddie, who was now trembling all over, looking very faint. She put her arm around his shoulders to steady him.

"I can't believe it," Eddie muttered, shaking his head. "I killed a man. I killed him."

"We *have* to take off," Scott insisted, staring down the highway. "Now!"

"We can't do anything for this guy," Winks said from the side of the car. "It was a terrible accident. We'll live with it forever."

"Forever," Eddie repeated, staring down at the corpse.

"But we can't let it ruin our lives," Winks continued. "Come on. Get in!"

"I don't know," Cassie said, her mind spinning, the yellow beams of light suddenly growing brighter, then dimmer, as she stared at them.

She saw the black tire track on the white fluffball.

She felt so guilty.

It took her a while to realize that the others were staring at her, waiting for her to decide.

"Okay," she said with a loud sigh. "Let's go."

"Brandt Tinkers," Eddie said, staring at the corpse. "Brandt Tinkers."

"Eddie, come on," Cassie urged, guiding him to the car, her hand gently on the shoulder of his down vest.

"Do you think he has a family?" Eddie asked, not moving.

"Hurry!" Winks cried. "Someone will come along. We've been lucky so far."

"Who's going to drive?" Scott asked.

"Not me!" Eddie cried. "I can't!"

"Then I'll drive," Winks said and jumped behind the wheel, immediately slamming the door after him.

"But we can't just leave him lying in the middle of the highway!" Cassie protested, not recognizing her shrill, frightened voice.

"Help me move him," Scott said, stepping close to her. "Are you okay?" he whispered.

She nodded. "I guess. I don't know."

"We'll carry him to the side of the road," Scott said, staring into her eyes.

"No! Don't touch him!" Eddie screamed.

"Let's get Eddie to the car first," Cassie suggested to Scott. "He's not doing too well."

They each took an arm and walked Eddie to the car. He sagged down in the back seat, crossing his slender arms protectively over his chest, staring down at the floor. Then Cassie and Scott quickly rolled the corpse onto the grassy shoulder of the road.

"I've never touched a dead man before," Cassie said, shuddering, suddenly chilled from head to foot.

Scott put an arm around her shoulders. "Neither have I."

Leaning against each other, they made their way quickly to the car. Winks started up the engine before Cassie and Scott were inside. As soon as they had pulled their doors shut, he sped off, flooring the gas pedal so that the car lurched forward, throwing all of its passengers back against their seats.

"Winks, slow down!" Cassie scolded. "That's all we need is to get a speeding ticket!"

For some reason, this struck Scott as funny. He started to laugh his high-pitched giggle.

Winks laughed, too, high-pitched, nervous laughter. But he slowed the car down to forty.

"Eddie — feeling a little better?" Cassie asked, beside him in the back seat.

Eddie stared straight down.

"Eddie?"

"I guess," he said finally, not looking at her. "This is hit-and-run, you know. We could all be arrested."

"No one saw us," Winks said, slowing even more as they reached town, darkened stores passing on both sides. "No one. There was no one around."

"But we could all be arrested," Eddie insisted.

"We'll be okay," Cassie said softly. "Winks is right, Eddie. There were no witnesses. What happened is terrible. But it was an accident. An accident. You have to keep telling yourself that."

"What was Brandt Tinkers doing there in the middle of the highway, anyway?" Winks asked. He was starting to sound a little more like himself. He slowed and turned the car onto Market Avenue, still jammed with Saturday night traffic.

"He was just standing there in the road," Cassie said thoughtfully.

"And I killed him," Eddie said, shaking his head.

"Stop it, Eddie," Cassie said softly. "We've got to go on, you know. We've got to go on as if nothing happened."

"But how *can* we?" he wailed.

"We have no choice," Scott said firmly, turning to look at Eddie from the front seat.

"In a way, we were lucky," Winks said, sliding his hands nervously back and forth on the plastic steering wheel. "I mean, no one came by that entire time. Not a car. Not a truck. Nothing."

"Yeah, lucky," Eddie muttered.

"Winks is right, Eddie," Cassie said, finding herself becoming a little impatient with him. "There were no witnesses. That was really lucky."

Winks pulled the Chevy to the curb in front of Eddie's house.

There, hunkered on the front stoop, illuminated by the light from inside the open front door, stood two blue-uniformed policemen.

7
Act Natural

"Keep driving! Keep driving!" Eddie cried, leaning forward, grabbing the back of Winks's seat and shaking it with both hands.

"I can't!" Winks told him. "They've already seen us. Look!"

All four teenagers looked at the house. The two policemen, one tall and rangy, the other squat and overweight, had turned away from the front door and were staring expectantly across the yard at them, hands on hips.

"They're going for their guns!" Eddie cried, his face pressed against the car window.

"No, they're not," Cassie assured him. "They're waiting for us to get out."

"Come on. Let's go," Scott said, reaching for his door handle.

"How did they find out?" Eddie wailed, not moving. "How did they get here so quickly?"

"Just act natural," Winks advised, cutting the headlights, then turning back to Eddie as he opened the car door. "Act natural. You can do it, man."

Eddie didn't reply.

"Take a deep breath and count to ten," Cassie instructed him. "Then come out."

She waited for him to follow her advice. Then she followed him out of the car.

The two policemen had walked halfway down the small, treeless yard to greet them. "Hey, how's it going?" the short one called amiably.

The four teenagers stood in a row at the curb, trying to look calm, trying to look normal.

"Any of you live here?" the squat policeman asked. The tall one took off his blue cap, then rearranged it on his blond hair.

"I do," Eddie muttered.

Cassie could feel him trembling beside her.

The two policemen ambled together the rest of the way down the sloping front yard until they were standing about two feet in front of the four friends.

"How long you been away?" the tall one asked Eddie, glancing at the car behind them.

"Not long," Eddie said, shifting his weight awkwardly. "A few minutes."

"Is there a problem?" Winks asked, nervously pushing up his glasses.

"Huh-uh," the tall policeman said, turning his gaze on Winks. "Just that we saw the front door wide open, and no car around, so we thought we'd check."

Scott giggled, relieved. The others remained silent.

"I must've forgot to shut it," Eddie said, glancing at Cassie. "We just went to McDonald's."

"You must've been hungry," the short policeman said, snickering.

His partner remained somber-faced. "You should always lock the door. Especially on Saturday night. It's a bad night for break-ins."

"Thanks," Eddie said, forcing a smile. "That was really nice of you to stop."

The police radio blared suddenly in the patrol car, which was parked across the street. The tall policeman touched the brim of his cap. "Have a nice night," his partner said. The two of them hurried to their car and sped away.

Cassie, Scott, and Winks went inside with Eddie. They spent nearly an hour reassuring him, calming him down, getting him to promise he wouldn't tell anyone about the accident. Then they wearily walked to their homes.

Cassie was pleased to see that her parents had already gone to bed. She really didn't feel like making small talk with them, having to lie about how she spent the evening.

"Oh, we took Eddie's parents' car out for a ride

and ran over a man. Yes, he died. But don't worry, Mom and Dad, no one saw us."

Oh, that would go over real big, wouldn't it? Cassie thought ruefully.

Real big.

It took her a long time to fall asleep and when she finally drifted off, she dreamed she was driving.

Driving and driving and driving down an endless dark road.

She didn't know where she was headed.

She wanted to stop, but she couldn't.

She was lost, she knew. Terribly lost. Surrounded by swirling blackness.

She couldn't stop driving. She had to follow the road wherever it went.

And the road was so bumpy.

So many bumps. Big bumps.

The car was bumping up and down, each bump bouncing her head against the roof with a hard jolt.

Bump bump bump.

So many bumps in the road.

Were the bumps all bodies? she wondered as she drove.

Could she really be driving over so many bodies?

If only she could stop. . . .

But there was no way.

She woke up bathed in sweat, and squinted at the alarm clock beside her on the bed table. Five-twelve.

So early.

But she knew she couldn't get back to sleep.

She didn't feel at all rested. The dream was still vivid in her mind. The endless, black road. The bumps in the road.

"Ohhh," she moaned aloud, and wondered if her three friends were awake, too.

Poor Eddie.

Eddie Katz. Scaredy Katz.

Well, he had reason to be scared now, didn't he? Didn't they all?

No, she decided.

It'll take a while to forget. But it's over.

Over.

The dead man's face loomed up in her mind, but she quickly forced it away.

The Cubs cap. The blue-and-red Cubs cap lingered in her thoughts. And then she saw the gray, staring eyes again.

Accusing her. Accusing them all.

Well, she decided, it's going to be harder than I thought to force the hideous pictures out of my mind. It'll take time. Maybe a lot of time.

But I'm going to do it.

It's over. Over.

Just a nightmare. Like my bumpy-road nightmare.

But now it's over.

She stayed in bed, wide awake, until she heard

her parents rustling about downstairs. Then she got
dressed quickly, pulling on a pair of gray sweat-
pants and matching sweatshirt. She checked herself
out in the mirror and was surprised to see that she
looked exactly the same.

Her green eyes stared back at her inquisitively.
I feel so different, she realized. I feel like an entirely
different person. How weird that I should still look
like the old me.

She pushed at her blonde, crimped hair until it
looked a little less disheveled, then headed down to
breakfast.

"What did you do last night?" her mother greeted
her from the breakfast table, a steaming cup of cof-
fee in her hand.

"Not much," Cassie said.

The Sunday paper had nothing in it about a hit-
and-run killing on Route 12. Cassie listened to the
radio that afternoon and watched a local TV news-
cast at six. Still no report.

Is it possible that the man's body hasn't been
found? she wondered.

There wasn't a whole lot of traffic on Route 12.
But, surely anyone passing the Hanson Underpass
would see a man's body lying on the side of the road.

Puzzled, she called Scott, but he couldn't talk.
His parents were standing right there.

Monday morning, Cassie hurried to the front

porch in her nightshirt, and unrolled the newspaper, certain that the story would be in it by now.

Shivering in the morning cold, she quickly scanned the headlines. There were reports of three different traffic accidents in Avondale, and two others just north of the city. But no story about a body being found; no story about a hit-and-run murder.

Murder.

Shivering from more than the cold, she hurried inside and slammed the door.

That night after dinner, Cassie told her parents she was going over to Scott's to study. But as she walked to Scott's house, she knew there was no way they could concentrate on their homework.

"What is going on?" she asked in a low whisper when she and Scott had finally managed to be alone in the den. "It's like the body *vanished* or something." She tucked her legs under her on the red leather couch.

"Maybe no one found it," Scott suggested, pacing back and forth in front of her. "Maybe it's still lying there."

"For two days? In broad daylight?" Cassie asked, forgetting herself and raising her voice.

Scott put a finger to his lips and glanced toward the den door.

"Don't worry. Your parents just think we're making out," Cassie said. "They won't come in."

Scott giggled mirthlessly. "You're right. They

would never suspect we're talking about a murder."

"An accident," she corrected him. "Don't start talking like Eddie."

"How's Eddie doing?" Scott asked.

Cassie shrugged. "I haven't seen him."

"Do you want to try and study?" he asked, leaning heavily against an oak bookshelf.

Cassie shook her head. "I want to drive out to that spot on Route 12 and see if he's still lying there."

"No way," Scott said, making a face.

"Why not?" she demanded.

"In whose car? My parents are home, remember? We can't say 'Give us the car keys. We're going for a ride. See you later.' "

"We could sneak out," Cassie suggested.

"Don't be lame," Scott said sharply. "We couldn't back one of the cars down the driveway without them hearing it." He sighed and pushed himself away from the bookcase. "Listen, Cassie, it's a good thing there've been no news stories."

She stared up at him. "Why do you say that?"

"It means no one is looking for us. We're not in any trouble." He stretched his arms, arching his back, reaching up toward the low, paneled ceiling, his sweatshirt riding up on his stomach.

"How can you be sure?" Cassie asked.

A knock on the door interrupted the conversation.

"What is it, Mom? We're studying," Scott said irritably.

But the door opened, and Eddie walked in. "Hope I'm not interrupting anything." His face turned beet red.

"We're just talking," Cassie said. She motioned for him to close the den door. Across the hall in the living room, Scott's parents were watching some sitcom on TV.

"What's happening?" Eddie asked, glancing at Scott, then Cassie, as he walked toward the couch.

Cassie scooted over to make room for him. The color was fading from his face, but his cheeks were still pink.

"Cassie's all pushed out of shape because our . . . accident hasn't been on TV or anything," Scott said quietly.

"Me, too," Eddie confessed. "It's so weird, isn't it?"

"I want to drive out and see if the body is still there," Cassie said.

Eddie's breath seemed to catch in his throat. He coughed. "Not me," he said finally. "I'm not going back there."

"But aren't you curious?" she demanded. "Don't you want to know if the body was found?"

"No," Eddie said. "I've been forcing the whole thing out of my mind. At least, I've been trying to. I don't want to go back there. I really don't, Cassie.

It'll make me see it all over again. It'll make it fresh again. I won't go. I won't."

"Whoa. Hold on," Scott said sympathetically. "Cool your jets, man. We're not going back there. None of us."

Cassie's face filled with disappointment. "What *are* we going to do? Nothing?"

"Yeah," Scott said. "Nothing." He stopped short. Then stared at Eddie. "I just got an idea," he said. "Eddie, what about your cousin?"

Eddie looked up from the couch, confused. "Jerry?"

"Yeah. Your cousin Jerry. The one who works at the morgue."

"What about Jerry?" Eddie asked. "He wouldn't know why a story didn't get in the newspaper."

"No. But he'd know if the body was found — wouldn't he?" Scott asked excitedly.

"Right!" Cassie cried, jumping up from the couch. She walked over to the desk and picked up the phone. "Here, Eddie — call him."

"But — wait — " Eddie protested.

"Just ask him if someone named Brandt Tinkers was brought in," Cassie said, shoving the phone receiver into his hand.

"And what do I say if Jerry asks me why I want to know?" Eddie demanded, staring unhappily at the phone.

"You'll think of something," Cassie said, "Quick — dial."

"Wait," Scott said, moving in front of Cassie and pushing a button on the phone. "Let's put it on the speaker phone so we can all hear."

"I don't have the number," Eddie whined, reluctantly taking the phone from Cassie. "And I don't know if Jerry works Monday nights."

"It's worth a try," Scott said, leaning over the desk, hovering beside Eddie.

"Oh . . . all right," Eddie said grudgingly. He called Information and got the number for the city morgue. Then he punched in the number.

Leaning in close, all three of them listened to the ring on the speaker phone. They listened to the hoarse voice of the receptionist. Then a few seconds later, Eddie's cousin Jerry came on the line.

They "How's-it-goinged?" each other for a minute or so. Then Eddie got to the point and asked Jerry if a dead man named Brandt Tinkers had been delivered to the morgue.

"Yeah," Jerry replied, his voice rising with surprise.

Cassie gasped.

The three of them glanced at each other, then stared straight ahead at the speaker phone.

"Yeah," Jerry repeated. "The cops brought him in late Saturday night. Still warm. A hit-and-run. He was crushed up really bad. They found him out on some highway. You know the guy, Eddie?"

"No. No, Jerry," Eddie uttered weakly.

"He's a businessman. Some kind of banker or

something," Jerry continued. "The family is keeping the whole thing quiet. To help the cops. I guess the cops are working real hard to find out who ran over the guy." Jerry paused.

The silence seemed heavy.

"That's all I know, Eddie," he continued finally. "How'd you hear about this guy? It hasn't been in the paper or anything."

"Oh . . . I know a kid who knows the guy's kid," Eddie lied, staring at Cassie as he said it.

When he got off the phone, Eddie's face was filled with fear. "Did you hear what Jerry said?" he asked. "He said the police are after us. We're going to be caught. I just know it!"

And at that moment, they heard a hard pounding on the front door.

8

A Disappearance

Scott tore open the den door and raced through the front hallway to the door. Cassie and Eddie followed reluctantly behind.

"Don't run!" Scott's dad called, appearing from the living room. "What's your hurry, guys? It sounded like a cattle stampede."

It's the police, thought Cassie.

How did they find us so quickly? And how did they find us here at Scott's house?

Scott pulled open the door. "Oh. Hi, Mr. Olson." Scott sounded almost disappointed. It was his next-door neighbor, a bald, friendly-looking man with crinkly blue eyes. He was holding a red metal tool-box by the handle.

Scott pushed open the storm door.

Mr. Olson stepped into the entryway, stamping his feet on the doormat. "Just wanted to return

61

this," he said, talking to Mr. Baldwin over Scott's shoulder.

"Thanks. Come in, Ed," Scott's dad said, squeezing past the three teenagers to take the box from his neighbor.

Cassie, Eddie, and Scott made their way back to the den.

"That was crazy," Scott said, carefully closing the door.

"I really thought it was the police," Cassie said, slumping back onto the leather couch.

"We've got to calm down. We've *got* to," Scott said heatedly.

"But how *can* we?" Eddie cried, his cheeks bright scarlet. "I *killed* a man!"

"There was no reason to think that was the police," Scott said, keeping his voice low. "The police aren't going to find us. They haven't got a clue. So we've got to stop driving ourselves crazy."

"Scott's right," Cassie said quickly.

Eddie was standing by the window, staring out at the house next door. It was obvious to Scott and Cassie that he hadn't heard a word they'd said. He was off somewhere in his own world, a frightened, confused world.

"I know what I'm going to do," Eddie said suddenly, very softly, not turning around.

"What?" Cassie asked.

"I'm going to turn myself in."

"No, you *can't!*" Cassie insisted, jumping up from

the couch and joining Eddie by the window.

He didn't look at her. Instead, he pressed his forehead against the cool glass. His entire face, she saw, was flaming red.

"You can't," Scott echoed. "We're all in this together, Eddie."

"I was driving," Eddie said, pressing his face against the glass.

"But we were all there," Cassie told him. "We all decided to leave rather than stay and face the consequences. We all were there without a license. All of us."

"If you turn yourself in, you're turning *us* in, too," Scott said.

"No," Eddie insisted, spinning around to face Scott. "I'll tell them I was alone. I'll tell them I took the car myself. There was no one with me. They'll believe that. No reason not to."

"Don't," Cassie pleaded, putting a hand on Eddie's slender shoulder. "Don't mess up your life. Wait a few days, Eddie."

"Cassie's right," Scott said. "Wait a few days. It'll all blow over. You'll feel better. We all will. I know it."

They led Eddie to the couch and sat him down between them. They talked to him for more than half an hour, calming him, reassuring him, pleading with him not to go to the police.

"We just have to wait this out," Cassie said sympathetically. "Sure, it's rough, Eddie. It's roughest for you since you were driving. But you've got to keep remembering that we're all in it together, and we're all with you."

"I keep thinking this is just one of Winks's horrible practical jokes," Eddie said sadly, his hands clasped together tightly in his lap. "I keep thinking that any minute, Winks is going to laugh and yell, 'Gotcha!' " He closed his eyes. "But it isn't a joke," he said softly. "It isn't a joke."

Scott went to the kitchen and returned a few minutes later with three Cokes and a bowl of potato chips. Setting the tray down on the big oak desk, he glanced at Cassie, who returned his glance with a faint smile.

At least we've talked Eddie out of going to the police, her expression told Scott.

The phone rang. Scott picked it up.

The speaker phone was still on. All three of them heard Jerry's voice. "Is Eddie there? His parents said he was with you."

"Yeah, I'm here, Jerry," Eddie called. "What's wrong?"

"Well, you won't believe this, Eddie," Jerry said. "I just had to call you back."

"What's going on?" Eddie asked, his expression tight with worry. Scott and Cassie froze, listening intently to the voice coming through the small speaker.

"You know that corpse you called me about? That Tinkers corpse."

"Yeah, Jerry. Yeah?" Eddie couldn't hide his impatience.

"Well, the corpse was here when I talked to you," Jerry continued, sounding baffled. "But it isn't here now."

"Huh?" Scott cried, leaning over the phone.

"It disappeared, man," Jerry said. "Gone. I mean, like it got up and walked out."

9

A Message from the Dead

Tuesday morning, Cassie found it impossible to concentrate in class. Mr. Miller called her name three times before she realized he was talking to her. Everyone laughed.

She felt as if she were surrounded by fog. Her friends and classmates appeared to be drifting, their smiling faces far away in the mist, their voices distant and muffled.

She had lunch in the cafeteria, finding a spot at a corner table with Scott and Eddie.

"What *is* that on your plate?" Scott asked, pointing with his fork at the yellow-and-white substance.

"Macaroni and cheese, I think," Cassie said, making a face. "I should've just taken an apple or something."

"What happened in Miller's class this morning?" Eddie asked. "He practically stood on his head to get your attention."

Cassie shrugged. "Just thinking about things," she said, mushing her fork around in the macaroni but not lifting any to her mouth. "I didn't hear him call me."

"Didn't sleep last night?" Scott asked. "You should've called me. I was up, too."

"I guess none of us are sleeping too well," Eddie said, gazing at the ham sandwich his mother had packed for him. He raised his eyes to Cassie. "I keep thinking about that corpse disappearing."

"Don't think about it," Scott said curtly. He took a big bite of his turkey sandwich. Mayonnaise ran down his chin.

"Jerry was really freaked out about it," Eddie said.

Cassie gingerly tasted the macaroni. It wasn't bad. She took another forkful.

"Know what I keep thinking?" Eddie asked, his cheeks reddening.

"Can we change the subject?" Scott demanded, glaring at Eddie impatiently. "It's enough already. We're okay, Eddie. There's no problem. It's time to stop talking about it."

"Give him a break, Scott," Cassie said quietly. "Why are you so pushed out of shape this afternoon? Let Eddie talk."

Scott scowled at her and rolled his eyes.

"Know what I think?" Eddie repeated, ignoring Scott's impatience. "I think this sounds like something Winks would do."

"Huh?" Scott's mouth dropped open, revealing a white gob of chewed-up turkey.

"You mean steal the corpse?" Cassie asked, not understanding.

"Yeah." Eddie nodded. "Don't you think?"

Cassie and Scott didn't reply immediately.

"I mean, he's always playing really mean jokes on me," Eddie said, nervously folding and unfolding his lunch bag. "He just thinks it's a riot to embarrass me, or make me squirm and feel like a total fool."

"Whoa," Scott said, holding up a big hand as if to hold Eddie back. "Winks just likes practical jokes, that's all. He does it to everyone."

"That's not true," Eddie replied sharply. "I'm his number-one victim, and you know it."

"I don't think Winks would go this far," Cassie interrupted softly, hoping to stop their argument before it got out of control.

"Hey, Katz! Scaredy Katz!" a boy named Gary Franz called from a table across the room. A milk carton came flying onto their table, landing in Cassie's macaroni.

Cassie grabbed it, jumped to her feet, and angrily prepared to heave it back. But Miss Meltzer, the lunchroom monitor, was staring at her from the center of the room.

Cassie sat back down. She heard raucous laughter from Gary Franz's table. "He's a creep," she muttered, tossing the milk carton aside.

"Everyone gives me a hard time," Eddie said,

almost mournfully. "But Winks started it. He was the first one to call me Scaredy Katz. And he's the only one who — "

"Winks might take an eyeball," Cassie interrupted, gesturing for Eddie to calm down, "but I don't think he'd take an entire *corpse*."

"No way," Scott said, shaking his head. "Why would he do it?"

"Just to scare me," Eddie replied. "He would. I know he would."

"Well," Scott said thoughtfully, "there's only one way to find out."

Cassie and Eddie stared back at him.

"Ask him," Scott said. "We'll go ask him."

They didn't see Winks all afternoon. After school, Cassie and Eddie hung around doing homework in the library while Scott had wrestling team practice in the gym.

Scott emerged a little before five, red-faced and weary, his blond hair wet and matted down on his head. He tossed his backpack over the shoulders of his bulky blue-and-gold letter jacket and led the way out the front door of the school.

"Coach gave us a real workout," he explained. "Had us doing laps all afternoon. Good conditioning, I guess. But I didn't sign on for track — I signed on for wrestling."

"Poor boy," Cassie said in a tiny voice, patting him on the back with mock sympathy.

Eddie scurried to keep up with them, walking in thoughtful silence.

It was a damp, gray day. The whole world seemed to be laid out in shades of gray. No color anywhere to be seen.

They walked to Winks's house, not saying much.

Winks pulled open the front door, a startled expression on his face. "A surprise?" he exclaimed. "Is it my birthday already?"

No one laughed.

"What's wrong?" Winks asked, turning serious.

"Can you come out for a while?" Cassie asked, seeing Winks's mom hovering behind him in the hallway. "Hi, Mrs. Winkleman," she called, waving to her.

Winks's mom waved back and called out a greeting.

"I can't," Winks said softly. "I'm — I'm kind of grounded. In fact, you guys have to go."

"Grounded?" Eddie asked suspiciously. "How come?"

Winks turned to check behind him. His mother had disappeared into the kitchen. "The eyeball," he said, making a sour face. "I took it home. My mom was cleaning my room and — "

Scott giggled. "She found it?"

Winks nodded.

Everyone laughed.

"It's not funny," Winks said. "She nearly lost her

lunch. I meant to get rid of the thing. It didn't keep too well. You could practically die from the smell alone. Anyway, when I got home, she shoved the box into my hands. And asked me to explain what it was doing in my room."

"What did you tell her?" Cassie asked.

"I said it was for a science experiment," Winks replied. "For extra credit. But she didn't buy it. She grounded me." Hearing footsteps, he looked behind him. "You guys have got to go."

He started to close the storm door, but Eddie pulled it back open. "Winks — did you take the corpse from the morgue?" he asked.

"Ssshhh!" Winks raised a finger to his lips and checked behind him once more. "Why don't you let the whole neighborhood hear, Katz?"

"Did you?" Eddie repeated, a little softer. "Did you take the body?"

"Yeah. I've got him up in my room," Winks replied.

"Huh?" Scott cried.

Cassie and Eddie stared at Winks in surprise.

"That's a joke, guys. An eyeball is enough. You know?" Winks shook his head. "It got me in enough trouble."

"You didn't take it?" Eddie repeated, unable to hide the suspicion from his voice.

"No way," Winks said heatedly. "I'm not a *ghoul*, Katz."

"*Who's* not a ghoul?" Mrs. Winkleman asked, appearing behind Winks in the doorway.

"I'm not," Winks said, flashing her a phony grin.

"Yes, you are," his mother said. "If you go by what you keep in your room. You're *definitely* a ghoul."

"Very funny, Mom," Winks said, sighing.

"We're all very funny in this family," she said, frowning at Winks. "You kids have to go, I'm afraid. Sorry to be rude. But the uncool ghoul here is grounded. That means no visitors."

"We were just going," Cassie told her.

"See you guys," Winks said.

"No, he won't," Mrs. Winkleman said, pulling the storm door shut.

"He doesn't have the corpse," Scott said to Eddie as they walked down the driveway. "You need a better theory."

"No, he doesn't," Cassie said. "No more theories, Eddie. No more ideas. No more thoughts about the missing corpse. Just force yourself to think about other things."

"Cassie's right," Scott said, putting his arm heavily around her slender shoulders as they crunched over the gravel. "It's all over. Done with."

"A done deal," Eddie said. "A done deal." But his expression remained thoughtful, his eyes on the gray distance.

That night, just after eleven, Cassie was struggling through her chapter in the government textbook, trying to get her eyes to focus on the blur of type, when the phone rang. She picked it up after the first ring. "Hello?"

"Is this Cassie Martin?" a woman's voice asked.

"Yes."

"This is the operator. I have a collect call for you from Brandt Tinkers. Will you accept the charges?"

Cassie nearly swallowed her bubble gum. Her mouth dropped open, but no sound came out.

"Will you accept the charges?" the operator repeated impatiently.

Brandt Tinkers?

What's going on here? Cassie wondered.

Her heart began to thud against her chest. Her hands went ice cold.

"Uh . . . yes. Okay," she managed to reply in a shaky voice.

"Go ahead, please," the operator said, and then clicked off.

Cassie heard crackling on the line.

"Hello?"

More crackling. And then a sound like a gasp, a dry gust of wind.

"You can't run away."

The voice wasn't a whisper. It was a breeze. A burst of air.

A burst of foul air.

"You can't run away."

And then the line went dead, leaving Cassie trembling and cold.

10
Hats Off to Eddie

"Cassie!"

Cassie slammed her locker on her finger. "Ow! Eddie, you scared me!"

"Sorry." His face turned crimson.

Cassie shook her hand hard, then sucked on the throbbing finger.

It was a little after eight-thirty on Wednesday morning. The bell for homeroom would ring in less than five minutes.

Eddie was wearing navy-blue corduroy slacks and a faded Bart Simpson T-shirt. He gazed at her with concern. "Is your finger okay?"

"Yeah, I always slam it in my locker to wake myself up," Cassie said sarcastically. Seeing the hurt look on his face, she softened her tone. "It's not broken."

"I got a phone call last night," Eddie said, leaning close and whispering confidentially.

74

"Hey, Katz — why don't you kiss her?" someone yelled, then laughed and disappeared around the corner.

"So did I," Cassie said, blowing on the still-painful finger. She was wearing an emerald-green sweater that matched her eyes and made her blonde hair seem to glow. Using her good hand, she straightened the hem of the sweater, pulling it down over the faded denim miniskirt she wore over heavy black tights.

"What — do you think?" Eddie stammered, staring hard into her eyes, as if trying to read her thoughts.

"I think it was some stupid practical joker," Cassie said angrily.

Eddie's face fell in disappointment.

Cassie snickered. "Come on, Eddie, you didn't really think it was a dead man calling, did you?"

He avoided her stare.

"You really are gullible," Cassie muttered, then immediately regretted it when she saw his features tighten and his face redden. "It had to be a joke, Eddie," she said, putting a hand on his shoulder.

"But who?" he asked, in almost a plea.

She shrugged. "It sure as heck wasn't Brandt Tinkers."

The bell rang. Cassie lifted her backpack to her shoulder.

Eddie didn't move. "The voice on the phone said, 'You can't run away.' "

"Same as my call," Cassie said, turning her eyes down the rapidly emptying hall.

"And then he said, 'I know you were driving,' " Eddie told her.

Her mouth formed a small O of surprise. Then she shook her head as if shaking it all out of her mind. "Just a stupid joke. Someone being dumb."

"But the four of us — we're the only ones who know," Eddie said.

"We're going to be late," Cassie said, staring down the empty corridor. Classroom doors were closing all down the hall.

"I don't care!" He grabbed her shoulder. "I — I can't think about class. This is just too weird, Cassie, too creepy."

"What are you going to do?" Cassie asked. His hand was cold through her sweater. She could see that he was trembling.

He really is a scaredy-cat, she thought, and then silently scolded herself for being so cruel.

"I'm going to cut this morning," Eddie said. "Come with me?"

"No," Cassie replied, pulling away from his grip. "I can't. I mean, I don't want to. We have to go on with our lives, Eddie. As if nothing happened. We have to."

"Please?" he asked, pleading with her with his solemn dark eyes.

"No. And you shouldn't cut, either. Come on. Come to homeroom. Please."

The second and final bell rang. Cassie saw the door to her homeroom close. She shifted her backpack and began jogging toward it, her sneakers thudding loudly on the hard floor.

"Eddie, come on!" she called, her voice echoing in the empty corridor.

But he shook his head. Then he turned and disappeared around the corner.

What's he going to do outside by himself? Cassie wondered. Is he just going to wander around all day, having morbid thoughts, scaring himself even more?

As she opened the door and hurried to her seat, she felt guilty for a moment. I should have gone with Eddie, she thought. He asked for my help, and I refused.

She settled into her seat, let the backpack drop to her feet, and glanced up to the front row where Scott sat. He grinned back at her. He was wearing a hideously bright, fire-engine-red sweater. Cassie hoped he hadn't picked it out himself.

After attendance had been taken and a few announcements had been made, the bell rang for first period. Cassie picked up her heavy backpack and waited for Scott at the door as everyone piled out of the room.

"Hey, how's it going?" he asked cheerfully, deliberately bumping into her.

She caught herself against the wall. "Did you get a phone call last night?"

He shook his head. "From you? No, you didn't call me. Where were you?"

"No, not from me," she said, giving him a playful shove out the door. "A . . . scary phone call."

He shook his head again, his blond hair still wet from his morning shower.

"Eddie and I got weird phone calls," Cassie told him as they headed up the stairs to their first-period class.

"Me, too!" Winks cried, and grabbed each of them by a shoulder.

Cassie cried out in surprise. Scott, also startled, swung his body around, nearly toppling Winks down the stairs.

"You're dead meat, Winks," Scott said, making a fist. "Don't sneak up on me again!"

Winks ignored him. "I got a call, too, Cassie," he said, his face turning serious. "From the dead guy."

"What?" Scott uttered his high-pitched giggle.

"It isn't funny," Cassie snapped at Scott.

"Are you guys freaking out?" Scott asked.

They stopped at the top of the stairs. "What did he say to you?" Cassie asked Winks.

"He said, 'You can't run away.'"

"To me, too," Cassie told him. "He called Eddie, too."

"Weird you didn't get a call," Winks said to Scott. "You're the only one."

"Hey, you're blocking traffic!" someone yelled, bumping into Cassie.

The bell rang.

"Later," Scott said, starting to jog.

"Someone's trying to scare us," Winks said, following Cassie.

"They did a pretty good job scaring Eddie," she confided.

"So what else is new?" Winks exclaimed and, tossing his shaggy, brown hair, disappeared into the classroom.

Cassie had just finished helping her father with the dinner dishes when the phone rang. It rang once, then stopped. Her mother, she realized, must have picked it up in the other room.

"Cassie, it's for you!" Mrs. Martin called. "Don't talk too long. You said you've got a ton of homework tonight."

"I know, I know," Cassie muttered. She picked up the phone — and felt a heavy stab of dread in her chest.

Is it the dead man?

"Hello?"

"Hi, Cassie, it's me. Are you still eating dinner?" It was Eddie, sounding frightened, as usual.

"No. Just finished. I've got so much homework, I — "

"Cassie, come over. You've *got* to."

"Eddie, I can't," she insisted. "I just told you — "

"No. Please. Come over right now," Eddie said. Something in his voice told her she had no choice.

"Hi, Cassie. How've you been?"

"Hi, Mrs. Katz. I'm fine."

Eddie's mother was short and more than a little plump. She looked like a very round version of her son. She had the same blushing cheeks as Eddie, and the same black, curly hair, which she wore cut boyishly short. Even though it was only seven-thirty, she was already in a flannel nightgown and bathrobe.

"Aren't you feeling well?" Cassie asked, then felt foolish.

"Pardon this old bathrobe. I get so tired after work, I like to get comfortable," Mrs. Katz said, her cheeks reddening.

"Hi, how's it going?" Eddie asked, entering the tiny, hot living room.

"Okay," Cassie replied uncomfortably.

"Eddie said you two were going to study together," Mrs. Katz said, ushering Cassie over to the dinner table, which, since there was no dining room, occupied one corner of the living room.

"Oh, yeah. Right," Cassie lied, glancing at Eddie, as if to say, what's going on here?

"Well, come have some dessert before you start," Mrs. Katz said, pulling Cassie by the arm. "I made a cake. It's from a mix, but it's very moist. You like yellow cake?"

"Yes. Fine. I mean, thank you," Cassie stammered.

The three of them sat down and had slices of cake and cups of tea. Eddie kept staring meaningfully at Cassie. It was obvious that he was dying to tell her something.

But Mrs. Katz kept up a stream of conversation, and wouldn't take no for an answer after offering seconds on the cake.

"Mom, we've really got to start studying," Eddie said, his cheeks aflame, his second slice of cake only half-eaten.

"So who's stopping you?" she replied. She grinned at Cassie. "You liked the cake?"

"It was very good," Cassie said. "Very moist." She patted her stomach.

Mrs. Katz grinned. "So what are you two studying?"

"Math," Eddie said.

"Government," Cassie said at the same time.

"Oh, right. Government. Mom, we really don't have time to discuss it," Eddie said impatiently.

Mrs. Katz jumped to her feet, an offended look on her face. "Excuse me for living," she said sarcastically. "I was just trying to show an interest."

She gathered up the three plates and carried them into the tiny kitchen.

"Come upstairs," Eddie whispered.

Cassie followed him up the narrow, uncarpeted stairway, the stairs creaking under their feet. Eddie's room was the entire upstairs. It had been a storage space, but Eddie's dad had finished it off to provide Eddie his own room. Cassie had to duck her head. The ceiling was low and followed the sloping eaves.

"After dinner, I was carrying the garbage down to the street," Eddie said excitedly. "And look what I found hooked on the handle of the front door."

He pulled something out from under his bedspread and held it up for Cassie to see.

It was a red-and-blue Cubs cap.

Cassie gasped.

"There was a note tucked inside," Eddie said. He pulled it out of the cap and read it to her.

"My hat is off to the driver who killed me."

11
Hit and Run — Again

Saturday morning as Cassie was finishing her French toast, the phone rang. "Who would call this early?" Mrs. Martin, still in her nightgown and flannel bathrobe, asked.

"Only one way to find out," Cassie said. She lifted the receiver off the kitchen wall phone. "Hello?"

"I'm having a bad morning."

"Scott? What's your problem?" Cassie asked. She turned to her mother. "It's Scott."

"I dropped my toothbrush in the toilet," he said. Cassie laughed.

"Not so loud!" her mother pleaded, covering her ears. Mrs. Martin couldn't stand loud noises in the morning.

"You *what*?" Cassie exclaimed.

"You heard me," Scott replied grumpily. "I dropped my toothbrush in the toilet."

"How?"

"It wasn't easy," he muttered.

Cassie laughed again. "Did you really call this early just to tell me what an incredible klutz you are?"

"I'm sick, too, I think," Scott said, his voice hoarse and scratchy.

"You're definitely a sicko," Cassie joked.

"No. Really. I think I have the flu or something," he insisted. "I may not be able to meet you guys tonight."

"Boo-hoo." Cassie pretended to sob.

"You could at least be sympathetic," he snapped. "I mean, I'm sick, and I dropped my toothbrush in the toilet."

"Did you fish it out?" she asked.

"Not yet."

"Cassie, your French toast is going to be ice cold," her mother called from the table.

"I've got to go," Cassie said, turning her back on her mother. "I'm sorry about your toothbrush."

"What are you doing today?" he asked.

"Helping my dad. We're scraping the paint off the porch. So he can paint it."

"Thrills," Scott said.

"I promised him weeks ago," Cassie said.

"Cassie, your breakfast," her mother called.

"Call me later," Cassie said quickly. "Feel better."

She hung up and returned to the table. She

stabbed her fork into a square of French toast, dipped it in syrup, and raised it to her mouth. "Mom," she complained, "this French toast is ice cold!"

"Very funny," her mother said, rolling her eyes. "What did Scott want?"

"Nothing. He wanted to tell me he dropped his toothbrush in the toilet." Cassie wiped syrup off her chin with a paper napkin.

"You and those three guys certainly are close," Mrs. Martin said, staring at Cassie as if examining her.

"What's that supposed to mean?" Cassie asked edgily.

"Nothing. Not a thing," her mother replied quickly, raising both hands as if to hold Cassie back. "I just mean it's unusual for a girl your age to be so close with three boys."

"I don't think it's so *unusual*," Cassie said, pronouncing each syllable of unusual as if it were a foreign word. "They're nice guys."

"I didn't say they weren't," Mrs. Martin said defensively. "Let's just drop the subject, okay? I wasn't trying to get you upset."

"I'm not upset," Cassie told her. She shoved the plate away. She couldn't eat another bite. French toast for breakfast made her feel as if she weighed a thousand pounds.

The kitchen door opened, and her father came in, his face red from the cold, carrying two large brown shopping bags from Charlton's, a nearby lumber store. "I'm back," he declared.

"We can see that," Mrs. Martin said sharply. "Close the door. You're letting in the cold."

"I rented an electric sander, and I got a ton of sandpaper and a new plane," he announced.

"Does this mean you're serious about working on the porch?" Cassie asked, grinning. She knew it was a foolish question.

She and her father worked all morning and most of the afternoon. "I'll never get the paint dust out of my hair," Cassie complained, just after lunch.

"It looks good," her father joked, wiping the perspiration off his forehead with the sleeve of his sweatshirt. "Gives you some sparkle."

"I hate sparkle," Cassie replied.

As she worked, sanding the corners the electric sander couldn't reach, she thought about Eddie. The poor guy was just about having a nervous breakdown.

It had taken all of her convincing skills to keep him from calling the Avondale police and telling them about the accident. Scott and Winks had worked on him, too, reassuring him, explaining to him what a mistake it would be, and then, finally, pleading with him not to do anything, to wait it out.

On Thursday night, Eddie and Winks had received another phone call, supposedly from the corpse. This call was the same as the first — the dry, airy whisper of a voice over the crackling phone line. The same words — *you can't run away*.

So far, Scott was the only one who hadn't received a call.

Or a visit.

The red-and-blue Cubs cap flashed into Cassie's mind. It was so creepy holding it in her hand, running her fingers over the brim, stretching the elastic, knowing that it had been worn by a dead man.

A man they had killed.

Who left the cap on Eddie's door?

Who was making the calls?

Her suspicions had immediately fallen on Winks. But this was too ghastly, too cruel and sick, even for him. And, she saw Winks was just as frightened as the rest of them, even though he kept insisting that the accident was old news and that he didn't care about some joker making stupid prank phone calls.

Some joker.

Which joker?

Was someone on the Hanson Underpass that night? Had someone been standing on the old bridge when they hit Brandt Tinkers? Had someone witnessed the whole thing?

If so, it would have to have been someone who knew them, Cassie realized. Someone who recognized them, who knew where they lived, where to phone them.

And that was impossible.

The Hanson Underpass was miles out of town. There would be no reason for anyone they knew to be on that bridge that night.

What a mystery.

What a frightening, puzzling mystery.

"What are you thinking about?" Her father's voice interrupted her thoughts.

"Huh?"

"You looked a million miles away." He smiled at her, but his expression was apprehensive.

It had taken Cassie a while to come out of her thoughts, to realize that the whir of the electric sander had stopped, to see that her father was staring at her expectantly.

"Oh. Nothing," she replied. "Just thinking about school, I guess."

"When's your spring break?" he asked, turning his eyes to a spot on the ceiling he had missed.

"April," she told him. "First week in April."

"I'd like to plan a vacation," he said, moving the aluminum ladder. "For all three of us. Where'd you like to go?"

"Someplace far, far away," Cassie replied, without thinking.

She phoned Scott after dinner. He had the flu. He couldn't go out.

Cassie replaced the receiver, feeling disappointed. She knew she felt something more than friendship for Scott. She could tell he felt the same way.

In some strange way, the horrible accident and all that had followed had brought them even closer together, Cassie thought.

Wishful thinking?

She was pondering this when the phone rang in her hand, startling her.

The heavy feeling of dread weighed in again.

She felt it now every time the phone rang. It could be the dry, dead voice on the other end.

"Hello?"

"Hi, Cassie. It's me. Eddie."

"Are we meeting at the tenplex?" Cassie asked. "Did you check to see what's playing?"

"I — I'm not coming," Eddie said hesitantly.

"Huh?"

"I feel kind of bummed out," he said. "I'm just going to stay home and veg out. Watch the tube."

"Okay, Eddie." Cassie couldn't conceal her disappointment. After working all day, she really felt like going out. "You know, Scott's sick. Flu."

"My mom's got it, too," Eddie said. "Maybe that's why I feel so bummed out. Maybe I'm coming down with it, too."

"Hope not," Cassie said. "Talk to you tomorrow."

She hung up and groaned loudly. First Scott, then Eddie. I don't want to go out just with Winks, she thought. She liked Winks. But she mainly liked him when the others were around.

She decided to call him and tell him that no one felt like getting together, that she was going to stay home with her parents.

When she called, Mrs. Winkleman answered the phone. "Is that you, Cassie?" she asked. "Winks just left. I thought I heard him say he was heading over to your house."

"Oh. I see. I thought I'd catch him," Cassie replied. She thanked Mrs. Winkleman and hung up, trying to decide what to do.

What the heck, she thought. I'll go to the tenplex with Winks. I've got to get out of the house.

Winks lived five blocks away. She decided to start walking and meet him halfway. Pulling her down jacket out of the front closet, she yelled, "I'm going out! See you later!" to her parents and headed out the door.

It was a clear, cold night. Cassie glanced up at the full, white moon, zipping her jacket as she jogged down the drive.

She turned left, cutting across the Culbertsons' front yard, heading toward Winks's house, her sneakers thudding softly over the frozen ground.

Somewhere down the block, a little boy was calling to his mother.

He's out awfully late, Cassie thought. She glanced at her watch. It was only seven-thirty.

It's as dark as midnight, she thought, wishing winter was over.

A dog barked. A door slammed.

When she turned the corner onto Mulberry, she expected to see Winks.

The bright lights made her stop in surprise. She raised a hand to shield her eyes from the sudden glare.

What was going on?

The owners of the corner house, the Roths, had all of their front-yard floodlights on. The entire corner was bathed in harsh yellow light, brighter than daylight.

It took a while for Cassie's eyes to adjust to the brightness. When they did, she saw Mr. and Mrs. Roth and three of their children, huddled in the street.

None of them were wearing coats.

Cassie moved forward and saw something in the street.

A pile of clothing?

No. Someone was lying on the pavement.

And Mr. Roth was leaning over the person.

"Hey!" Cassie called.

She started to run.

The porch lights went on in the house across the street. A man came running down the driveway.

"Is he going to be okay?" Cassie heard one of the Roth kids ask. The little kid was crying. His mother picked him up.

"What happened?" Cassie asked, stepping up beside them. She looked down and gasped. "Winks!"

He was on his back, his head tilted at a strange

angle. His eyes were closed. There was blood on the front of his blue denim jacket.

"We called the ambulance," Mr. Roth told her. As he said this, they could hear sirens approaching from the distance.

"But what *happened?*" Cassie screamed, staring down at her unconscious friend.

"I was at the window," Mrs. Roth said. "He was walking at the curb. A car hit him. And then sped off."

"A hit-and-run," her husband said quietly.

12
Eddie Gets the Picture

The hospital walls were pea-soup green. The fluorescent lights on the low ceiling made everything — and everyone — look even greener.

What is that odor? Cassie wondered, stepping off the elevator and searching for the Intensive Care Unit. It smelled like medicine, like alcohol or ether or formaldehyde mixed with detergent, an odor found only in hospitals.

White-uniformed nurses passed by without looking at her. Two doctors in green lab coats were talking softly against a wall. The corridor was narrow, almost tunnellike. Cassie had to squeeze past them.

Down the corridor, past a deserted nurses' station, she saw Mrs. Winkleman, in a tan cloth coat, a big, black box of a pocketbook in her lap, sitting on a folding chair, her chubby hands clasping the handle of the bag tightly.

She didn't look up until Cassie was standing right in front of her. "Oh. Hi," she said. Her eyes were red. Her round cheeks revealed tear tracks running down both sides.

"What did the doctors say?" Cassie asked, standing awkwardly in front of Mrs. Winkleman's chair, trying to decide what to do with her hands. "Is Winks — ?"

"Still unconscious," Mrs. Winkleman said, avoiding Cassie's stare. Fresh tears formed in her eyes.

"But the doctors — ?" Cassie wasn't sure what to ask.

"I'm all alone," Mrs. Winkleman said, her voice in a whisper: "Dan is in Detroit. On business. I tried to call him, but he wasn't at his hotel."

"Would you like me to call him for you?" Cassie asked, eager to help in some way, any way.

Mrs. Winkleman shook her head. She wiped a tear from one eye with a finger.

"I'm sure Winks will be okay," Cassie said, realizing it sounded phony.

"He has some broken ribs. A broken arm. Some internal injuries," Mrs. Winkleman said. Her hands were pale white against the black pocketbook.

A cart went by, filled with small brown bottles, pushed by a white-smocked man with a grizzly white beard. He dipped his head in a nod as he passed by.

"Mrs. Roth saw the car. The car that hit him," Winks's mother said, her voice trembling. She sighed and wiped away another tear. "But she didn't know what kind of car it was."

"Did she — ?"

"She said it hit him and just kept going," Mrs. Winkleman said, shaking her head.

"How awful," Cassie muttered, crossing her arms protectively over her chest. It seemed about a hundred degrees in the hallway, but she still felt chilled.

"I can't believe it. I just can't believe it," Mrs. Winkleman said, sobbing.

"Where is Winks?" Cassie asked.

Mrs. Winkleman pointed to the door. And as she pointed, it swung open and a serious-faced young doctor with slicked-back brown hair, wearing a green surgical gown, stepped out.

"Mrs. Winkleman?" He spoke in a soft but deep voice.

Mrs. Winkleman jumped to her feet. "Is Bruce — ?"

"The internal injuries don't look serious," the doctor said, glancing at Cassie as he spoke. "We're encouraged. We're not certain we've stopped all the bleeding, though."

Mrs. Winkleman gasped.

"But we're keeping a close eye on him. We'll be monitoring him for the next couple of days."

"Is he awake? Can I see him?" his mother asked eagerly.

"Not yet," the doctor said somberly. "He hasn't

regained consciousness yet. It has us a little concerned. We did a brain scan. No sign of any problem there. It'll just take a little time. We're watching him. All of his vital signs are good."

Cassie stared at the doctor, trying to determine if he was telling the whole truth or if he was making Winks's condition sound better than it was. She decided the doctor had no reason not to be honest with Winks's mom.

"There's a waiting room just around that corner," the doctor told them, pointing. "You might be more comfortable there."

"No. I'll stay here," Mrs. Winkleman insisted. "If it's okay."

"Yes, it's okay," the doctor said, nodding to another green-gowned doctor who hurried past. "We'll let you know if there's any change in Bruce's condition."

He disappeared through the door to the Intensive Care Unit.

Mrs. Winkleman dropped back into the folding chair with a loud groan. "I can't believe it. I just can't believe it," she said, more to herself than to Cassie. "Saturday night, and look where I am."

"He sounded pretty encouraging," Cassie said. "He said — " She stopped, recognizing the two figures hurrying through the narrow, green corridor toward them.

"Eddie! Scott!"

The two boys, Eddie in his blue down vest, Scott

in a heavy wool parka, came up to her, their expressions set, squinting in the harsh, green light.

"How is he?" Scott asked eagerly.

"We don't know yet," Cassie told them.

"I just can't believe it," Mrs. Winkleman muttered, gripping and releasing the handle of her bag.

Scott turned away from them and sneezed violently. "Sorry," he said, searching his jeans pockets and pulling out a wad of tissues. "I'm really sick."

"You shouldn't have come," Cassie told him. "They don't want sick people in a hospital." What a bad time to make a joke like that, Cassie thought. What's *wrong* with me, anyway?

She was glad Scott had come, she realized. She was glad both boys had come. It helped her feel a little less alone, a little more like things were normal.

Normal?

She wondered what that word meant. She wondered if she would ever feel normal again.

"Where did it happen?" Eddie asked, unzipping his vest and leaning back against the wall.

"Just a few blocks from my house," Cassie said.

"He was walking to Cassie's," Mrs. Winkleman said quietly, glancing at Eddie. "One minute he was walking. The next minute . . ."

Cassie put a hand on her shoulder.

"Did the doctors say he'd be okay?" Scott asked.

"They don't know. He's still unconscious," Cassie said.

Eddie let out a gasp. "He isn't awake?"

Mrs. Winkleman shook her head. "The doctor said his brain is normal, thank God."

Normal, Cassie thought. There's that word again.

The door to the Intensive Care Unit opened, and two doctors walked out. "Any news about my son?" Mrs. Winkleman called as they passed by.

"No change," one of the doctors said brusquely, and the two of them continued down the hall.

Cassie and the two boys stayed with Mrs. Winkleman outside the Intensive Care Unit for another couple of hours. But when the doctor came out to report that Winks was stable but still not conscious, they decided they had to leave for home.

Scott was coughing and wheezing. Cassie felt his perspiring forehead. He definitely had a fever.

Eddie had pulled into himself like a frightened turtle. He had been silent the whole time, staring down at the floor. He seemed very relieved to be leaving, and practically ran to the phone booth to call his dad to come pick them up.

"Shall I drop you guys at your houses?" Mr. Katz asked as they piled into the old Chevy. He had to repeat the question. Being in the car again, the car that had hit and killed someone, gave both Cassie and Scott the creeps.

"Well, guys?" Mr. Katz repeated, a striped wool

ski cap covering his slender, bald head.

"Uh . . . bring them to our house, Dad," Eddie said. "That okay with you guys? We can talk a little."

Cassie really wanted to go home, but she recognized the panicky expression on Eddie's face. Realizing he needed their help, she reluctantly agreed. "Just for a few minutes," she told Eddie. "Scott has to go home and get back into bed."

Scott sneezed as if to demonstrate the truth of her words.

Mr. Katz asked about Winks, shaking his head, repeating again and again that he didn't think such a thing was possible in a quiet, peaceful community like North Avondale.

"Imagine. A hit-and-run," he said, pulling the car to the curb in front of their tiny house. "What kind of a person would do such a thing? Don't they have any kind of conscience at all?"

The three teenagers didn't reply. They glanced at each other, sharing the same thoughts, sharing the same memories, the same horrifying pictures flashing through their minds.

Eddie's shoulders shook. He looked about ready to confess to his dad that he was a hit-and-run driver, too.

We're *all* hit-and-run drivers, Cassie thought. We're all killers.

Eddie's father slammed the car door and went

running over the small square of a front yard and disappeared around the back. The three teenagers lingered at the curb.

"Poor Winks," Scott said, his voice a deep croak. He started to cough.

"A hit-and-run," Eddie said. "It couldn't be an accident."

Cassie's mouth dropped open. This was stretching things a bit far, even for Eddie. "Don't try to make this into more than it is," she warned Eddie. "It was an accident."

"No way," Eddie said, kicking at a clod of dirt with the toe of his sneaker.

"What are you saying, man?" Scott asked, wiping his nose with a tissue. "You think it *wasn't* an accident?"

Eddie didn't reply for a long while. "You tell me," he said finally in a low whisper. "You tell me. You think it's just a coincidence that we kill someone in a hit-and-run, and the next week Winks gets hit?"

"Yes, I think it's a coincidence," Cassie said heatedly. "Of *course* it's a coincidence. Don't be dumb, Eddie. It's one thing to be frightened. But don't get totally *dumb*."

He recoiled as if her words had stung him.

"I've got to get home. I feel like I'm dying," Scott moaned.

"A few more minutes," Eddie insisted. "Come inside. It's cold out here. I'll make you some tea. Come on. Please," he pleaded.

Scott glanced at Cassie. Cassie looked back at Eddie. "Hot tea would feel really good right now. I'm frozen." She pulled Scott by the arm. "Come on, sicko. Tea is what the doctor ordered."

They headed up to the house. And stopped on the front stoop under the bright porch light when they saw the large envelope tucked in the storm door.

"Oh, no," Eddie said quietly.

Cassie pulled the envelope out from the door. It was blank on both sides. No name or address. "What makes you think this is something terrible?" she asked Eddie.

"This is where I found the Cubs cap," he said, swallowing hard.

"That doesn't mean anything."

"Just open it up, will you?" Scott cried impatiently. "I really have to get inside. I'm shaking all over."

The envelope was sealed tightly. Cassie had trouble pulling it open. Finally, she ripped it, tearing along the top. Then she reached her hand in and pulled out a sheet of white, lined notebook paper.

"What is it? What's it say?" Eddie asked eagerly, his voice revealing his fear, leaning close over Cassie's shoulder.

She held the note up to the porch light. Scrawled in purple crayon were the words:

ONE DOWN, THREE TO GO.

"Oh, man," Scott said, shivering inside his big parka.

"I knew it," Eddie cried. "I knew what happened to Winks wasn't an accident."

Cassie stared at the words, reading them again and again until they blurred together, until they made no sense at all.

She grasped the envelope tightly. "There's something else inside it," she said.

Her heart thudding in her chest, she reached inside and pulled out a glossy, cardboard square.

A Polaroid photograph.

Cassie held it under the porch light. All three teenagers squeezed close together to stare at it.

"Hey, what's going on?" cried Scott, gaping at the Polaroid shot. "It — it *can't* be!!"

13
Cassie Figures It Out

The photograph slipped from Cassie's hand and fluttered off the stoop. Scott and Eddie both grabbed for it. Then Eddie dived off the stoop and scooped it up from the grass.

Even though it was no longer in her hand, Cassie still saw the horrifying image. It was an image she knew she would never be able to forget.

The Polaroid showed Scott's parents' car, the silver Volvo. The photo had been snapped to show the driver's side of the car. She knew it was Scott's silver Volvo because of the dark scratch on the driver's door.

Sitting behind the wheel, his head turned to face the camera, was Brandt Tinkers.

The corpse.

Smiling at the camera.

Sitting behind the wheel of Scott's parents' car.

So clear. The picture was so clear.

You could see that the corpse's eyes were sunk back in its head. You could see the purple tinge of its skin. The dark, unnaturally dark, lips.

The blank, unseeing stare as it faced the camera.

Sitting behind the wheel.

Of Scott's car.

Scott.

Cassie stared at Scott, who was trembling under the big parka, beads of perspiration on his forehead, his features drawn back in disbelief, in utter bewilderment as he stared at the photo, holding it close to his face with a trembling hand.

"I don't get it," Scott said, his voice hoarse. "I don't get it." He raised his eyes to Cassie. "This is impossible," he told her.

Cassie thought of Scott's new Polaroid camera, the one they had teased him about.

"I — I don't know how this happened," Scott said, suddenly realizing that both of his companions were staring at him. "Really. I have no idea."

Cassie believed him. She threw her arms around him, holding tightly to the parka, to show him that she did. "We have to get you home," she said softly. "Your face is so flushed. You're burning up."

"He's going to kill us all," Eddie muttered, still staring at the Polaroid, holding it close to his face under the porch light. "The corpse. He's going to kill us!"

"Eddie, stop!" Cassie cried.

"Well, who took this picture?" Eddie demanded,

staring at Scott. "How did the corpse get in Scott's car?"

"I don't know," Scott said weakly. "I'm telling you, Eddie — I don't know."

Suddenly the front door opened, startling all three of them. Eddie gasped and shoved the Polaroid into his vest pocket.

Mr. Katz pushed open the storm door. "What are you doing out there? You'll freeze your buns off. Are you coming in or not?"

"Uh . . . no thanks," Cassie said quickly. She took Scott's arm and tugged. "Come on. Got to get you home."

Eddie cast her a pleading stare, as if begging her not to leave. But enough was enough, Cassie decided. She wanted to get poor, sick Scott home. He seemed nearly dazed as she led him to the curb.

And she wanted to get home where she could think about everything quietly by herself.

Half an hour later, after depositing Scott like a heavy bag of laundry at his doorstep, and saying good-night to her parents, who were dozing off in the den with *Saturday Night Live* blaring on the TV, Cassie tucked herself into bed, turned off the bedtable lamp, and settled down on her pillow to think.

Staring up at the shifting shadows on the ceiling, like dark, playful ghosts over her head, she tried to put things in order, tried to step back and see things clearly.

But as much as she tried, her thoughts swirled about, much like the shadows she was staring at, one picture blurred into another, none of them as clear as the horrifying Polaroid of the corpse in the car.

Scott's car.

Scott's Polaroid?

No.

There were too many ugly pictures. Too many ugly questions.

Who had mowed Winks down? Who was trying to terrify them?

It couldn't be Scott. He was a big, lovable teddy bear. He wouldn't hurt a fly.

It couldn't be Eddie. He was too frightened, too scared of his own shadow, to pull anything this horrible.

And of course it couldn't be Winks.

So it had to be someone else. Someone who knew them. Someone they knew.

Someone who knew what had happened.

The corpse?

Cassie swallowed hard.

The corpse was the only other person who knew what had happened.

The dead man, Brandt Tinkers. There he was, crossing the highway when they hit him. There he was. Again, she saw his staring face caught in the headlights of the silver Volvo.

The corpse . . .

The only one who knows . . .

Before she realized it, Cassie had drifted off into a restless sleep.

A while later, she awoke suddenly, bathed in perspiration, the bedclothes twisted around her waist. Glancing at the bedtable clock, she saw that it was a little past three-thirty in the morning.

The ghostly shadows still swirled above her head.

Pale moonlight filtered in through the curtains on her window.

Only half-awake, Cassie sat up and took a deep breath.

And realized that she had figured it out.

She knew who was doing this to them.

14
A Visit to the Morgue

Before breakfast Sunday morning, Cassie called the hospital. After being transferred to three different nursing stations, she was told that Winks was still in stable condition, but that he hadn't regained consciousness.

No change from the night before.

Was that good news or bad news?

Cassie wished there were a doctor in her family, someone she could talk to about Winks, someone who could reassure her that he was going to be okay.

Still in her nightgown and robe, she punched Scott's number. His mother answered and said that Scott was too sick to talk. His temperature was 102 degrees, and he had terrible laryngitis, so he could barely make a sound. He had gone back to sleep, his mother said. She added that she'd probably keep him out of school the next day.

Cassie got dressed, pulling on a long-sleeved

green top over a pair of gray sweatpants. She pulled back the curtains and peered out of the window. The sky was a solid blue. The sun was shining. Across the street, the two Finnegan kids were chasing their big Irish setter across their yard.

A cheerful day, almost springlike. She pulled open the window, wishing she felt more cheerful.

She picked up the phone receiver and punched Eddie's number. A busy signal. She sat on her bed, staring at the billowing, white curtains, then tried again.

This time, Eddie picked up after the first ring. He had been trying to call the hospital, he told her, but hadn't been able to find out anything about Winks.

Cassie told him what she had learned from the nurse.

"I guess no change is good news," Eddie said.

"I guess," Cassie replied. "Listen, Eddie, does your cousin work on Sundays?"

The question seemed to catch him by surprise. "You mean Jerry?"

"Yeah. Jerry. The one who works at the morgue."

"I think so," Eddie said. "I could call him and find out. Why do you want to know?"

"I have a theory," Cassie said casually.

"You don't think Jerry has anything to do with what's going on, do you?" Eddie asked.

"Maybe," Cassie replied. "He's the only other

person who knows anything about the corpse. And he knows that you were interested in the corpse."

"But Jerry is a good guy!" Eddie exclaimed heatedly. "He wouldn't do anything like that. He wouldn't run down Winks. Jerry likes Winks!"

"Eddie — "

"Sure, Jerry likes to joke around sometimes. But you'd joke around, too, if you worked where he does." Eddie sounded very upset.

"Eddie, stop!" Cassie cried. "I'm not accusing your cousin of anything. He was the last person to see the corpse — right?"

"Right," Eddie reluctantly agreed.

"So I just thought maybe we could go talk to him."

"You mean go to the *morgue*?" Eddie cried, his voice rising several octaves.

"You don't have to come if you don't want to," Cassie said.

She didn't like the idea of going to the morgue, either. But she had an idea that Jerry might know what was going on, or be able to help them in some way.

"Uh . . . I'll call Jerry," Eddie said and hung up quickly.

Cassie pulled on her white Nikes and tied them tightly, then paced back and forth across her room, waiting for Eddie to call back.

I'm right about Jerry, she thought, pausing to peer out the window. The two Finnegan kids were wrestling in a mud puddle near the curb. The Irish setter was sitting on its haunches watching the bout.

Jerry knows something. Jerry has something to do with this.

Jerry is a bigger joker than Winks.

The phone rang. She dived to the bed and picked it up before the first ring had ended. "Hello?"

"Hi, it's me."

"Is Jerry at work?"

"Yeah," Eddie replied. "Jerry said that dead people don't take Sunday off."

"What a riot," Cassie said sarcastically. "Are you coming with me or not?"

"You mean you're just going over there? Right now?"

"Yeah. I'm taking the bus," she told him. "You coming?"

"I've got a lot of homework," he said.

"It won't take long," Cassie assured him.

"It's very cold in there," Eddie said, "and there are dead bodies all over the place."

"Big surprise! It *is* a morgue!" Cassie exclaimed, and laughed. She knew she shouldn't laugh at him, but he sounded like such a total coward.

He was silent for a long time.

"Eddie, are you still there?"

"I'll come with you," he said. "Meet you at the bus stop."

Cassie hung up and hurried down the stairs. Her

mom stopped her as she was heading out the front door. "Hold on — where are you going?" she asked, pulling Cassie back by tugging on her long, red wool scarf.

"Uh . . . just going to see Eddie," Cassie replied.

"Are you going to the hospital?" Mrs. Martin asked, brushing Cassie's hair back off her forehead.

"Maybe later," Cassie replied.

She had a sudden impulse to tell her mother she was going to the morgue.

She had a sudden impulse to tell her mother everything, to ask for help, to allow her mother to wrap her up in a protective hug and hide her.

"Your dad thought you might like to practice your driving today," Mrs. Martin said, rearranging the scarf around Cassie's neck.

"My driving?"

"Well, you *are* taking your driver's exam after school tomorrow," Mrs. Martin exclaimed. "Don't tell me you forgot. I thought you said it was the most important day in your life." Still holding on to the scarf, she stared suspiciously at Cassie.

How could I have forgotten about my driver's test? Cassie thought.

I've been so obsessed with Winks and the corpse and the horrid phone calls, I completely forgot!

"Of course I didn't forget," Cassie lied. "Tell Daddy I'll be home in a few hours. We can go driving then." She kissed her mom on the cheek and hurried out the door.

* * *

"Nice day," Eddie said, his hands shoved into his jeans pockets, his black hair still wet from the shower.

Cassie found him waiting for her on the corner, leaning against the blue-and-white bus pole.

"Nice day to visit the morgue," Cassie said dryly, watching an enormous crow hop along the sidewalk and onto the grass. "What's that — a buzzard?"

Eddie didn't laugh.

"Just trying to keep it light," she said.

"You want to go see Winks after the morgue?" he asked, his eyes on the crow. Another crow, identical in size, glided down beside the first one.

"I don't know," she told him, looking up to see the dark blue bus approaching. "My dad might take me driving. My test is tomorrow after school. I forgot all about it. Do you believe it?"

"My test is Friday," Eddie said, his cheeks reddening. He bent down, picked up a flat gray stone from the curb, took aim, and tossed it at one of the crows.

The stone hit the ground hard a few feet from the birds. They both squawked angrily and flapped up into the nearest tree.

The bus squealed to a halt. Cassie followed Eddie through the door. "Try to squeeze in," the bus driver joked. The bus was completely empty.

Cassie and Eddie walked all the way to the back. "Friendly, huh?" the driver called, watching them in the big rearview mirror. He pulled the bus away from the curb and headed toward the civic center.

"Have you ever been to the morgue before?" Cassie asked, watching the houses and yards roll past the window.

"Yeah. Once," Eddie said, resting his knees on the back of the seat in front of him. "Jerry showed me around. I had bad dreams for a month."

"Oh, great," Cassie said, rolling her eyes.

"This is a stupid idea," Eddie said. "Jerry isn't the one who ran down Winks. Jerry's just a goof. He isn't a killer."

The bus turned onto Civic Drive, its tires squealing. Up ahead through the windshield, some of the tall, new civic buildings, including the new state office tower, came into view.

"I just have this feeling we should talk to Jerry," Cassie said impatiently. "I told you, I don't think he's a killer."

"Well, don't tell him too much," Eddie said, his expression serious, staring hard into her eyes.

"Huh? Why not?" Cassie stared back at him.

"You know Jerry," Eddie replied quietly. "He makes a joke out of everything."

"Well, he won't joke about this," Cassie said. "I mean, Winks is in the hospital, and the rest of us have been threatened, and — "

"Just don't tell him too much," Eddie repeated.

They reached their stop. Eddie pulled the cord.

The bus pulled to the curb. "Y'all come back now, ya hear?" the bus driver called.

Cassie laughed as she stepped down to the curb. "Guess he's pretty lonely," she said.

Eddie's expression remained serious. "I wish we weren't doing this," he said, staring up at the gray office buildings.

Cassie ignored him and started walking. "Is that it, over there?" she asked, pointing to a low brick building, the only old building among all the new skyscrapers.

"Yeah," Eddie said, hurrying to keep up.

The new state office tower was made of enormous glass panels, and the glass reflected the sun back down to the street. Cassie shielded her eyes with one hand to shut out the bright glare as she crossed the street.

"It's deserted here," Eddie said, turning to look in all directions.

"No one works here on Sunday," Cassie said.

"Except Jerry," Eddie added.

Etched in a granite block beside the broad wooden entrance were the words: CITY MORGUE. 1952. Cassie tried the door, expecting it to be locked, but it pulled open easily.

They stepped into a wide, circular reception area, lit by one overhead light near the far wall. The reception desk, cluttered with papers and magazines, was unattended.

"I guess we can walk right back," Eddie said, whispering for some reason. "Jerry's area is way in back. With the stiffs."

He held back, allowing Cassie to lead the way. They walked through the empty reception area and into a long, narrow corridor with closed doors on both sides.

"Look out," Cassie warned, stepping carefully through the dark, narrow hall. "Hey — what's that?"

It was a stack of body bags, made of heavy, black plastic, piled in front of a closed office door. "They're empty," Eddie said, sounding very relieved.

Cassie shuddered. "They look like garbage bags, only they zip up."

The corridor led into a large, open room the size of a small gymnasium. There were metal examining tables in the center of the room, and what appeared to be wide, gray metal lockers built into all four walls.

"Hey, Jerry?" Eddie called. His voice echoed against the walls.

"At least there are no bodies just lying around," Cassie said, now whispering, too. "What is that sour smell?" She held her nose.

Eddie looked green. "Chemicals they use. Decaying bodies. It's all so disgusting."

Light poured in from narrow windows up near the high ceiling. They stepped into the center of the room, their sneakers thudding loudly on the concrete floor.

"Hey, Jerry! Where are you?" Eddie called.

Cassie stopped and uttered a shriek when she saw Jerry. She grabbed Eddie's hand and stepped back.

Eddie saw him, too.

Jerry was lying on his back on one of the low examining tables. His arms were crossed on his chest. His eyes were wide open, unblinking, staring lifelessly up at the ceiling. His head was surrounded by a wide pool of dark red blood.

15
Not Ticklish

"Jerry!" Eddie cried, and turned to Cassie, his face gripped with horror.

"This can't be happening!" Cassie exclaimed, holding on to Eddie's arm, squeezing it hard without realizing it.

"What can't be happening?" Jerry asked. He sat up, a wide grin crossing his face.

Cassie gasped.

"Gotcha," Jerry said and started to laugh.

Cassie and Eddie didn't join in. "Jerry, that wasn't funny," Eddie said, his voice just above a whisper. He sat down on the floor, his cheeks flushed. He looked about to faint.

"You really scared us," Cassie said angrily.

"Yeah," Jerry said, his grin growing even wider. He slid off the table and stood up. He held up the sheet of dark red cellophane that he had used for blood.

Jerry was tall and broad-shouldered, built like a fullback. He had long, frizzy blond hair that fell unbrushed around his round, usually grinning face. It was a mischievous face, Cassie thought. Jerry never looked serious. He had a diamond stud in one ear. He was wearing a faded blue work shirt, and gray denim, straight-legged jeans over black cowboy-style boots.

"I really thought — " Eddie started, but his voice caught in his throat, and he couldn't finish his sentence. He swallowed hard a couple of times, glaring angrily at Jerry.

"That was really unfair," Cassie said sharply. "You knew we'd be scared coming here and everything."

"Yeah," Jerry repeated, still grinning, enjoying his triumph. "Got to keep a sense of humor around here, you know. Otherwise, things get pretty dead." He snickered at his own bad joke.

Eddie, still sitting on the concrete floor, shook his head.

"So you guys want to see a corpse, huh?" Jerry asked. Without warning, he reached over to one of the wall lockers and pulled the handle.

"Jerry, stop!" Cassie pleaded.

But she was too late. A wide drawer slid out. On it, only partially covered by a white sheet, was the nude body of an old man.

"Come on, man, put it away!" Eddie screamed.

Jerry giggled.

"Yuck." Cassie felt sick. The smell was over-powering.

Jerry reached down to the dead man's feet. "Tickle, tickle." He tickled the sole of one foot. "Hey — not ticklish!" he cried, turning to Cassie and Eddie. "Here, want to try?"

"Jerry, *please!*" Cassie begged.

"Okay, okay," Jerry said grudgingly. He shoved the drawer. It clanged shut, the sound echoing off the high ceilings.

"It smells so gross," Eddie said, slowly climbing to his feet.

"You get used to it," Jerry replied. "It's not so bad after a while." He turned his attention to Eddie. "You okay?"

Eddie still looked shaky.

"Eddie doesn't like my jokes," Jerry told Cassie.

"Gee, what a surprise," Cassie replied sarcastically.

Jerry led them over to the desk in the corner. There were three wooden chairs lined up against the wall of lockers. They sat down.

"I heard about Winks," Jerry said, rubbing the back of his neck. "How's he doing? Have you heard?"

"He's still unconscious," Eddie said.

"I'm going over to the hospital later," Cassie added. "The doctor says he's stable, whatever that means."

Jerry *tsk-tsked* and shook his head. "Did they get the guy who hit him?"

"No," Cassie told him. "But something very strange — "

"We want to ask you something," Eddie interrupted, casting an uncomfortable glance at Cassie. "About the corpse."

"The one that's missing," Cassie said.

"Yeah. Wasn't that weird?" Jerry shook his head again. He pushed his frizzy blond hair back off his face.

"Do you know anything about the corpse?" Cassie asked.

"Huh-uh," Jerry said quickly, glancing at Eddie. "You sure you're okay? Can I get you a glass of water? Or maybe some formaldehyde?" He laughed, slapping the knees of his jeans.

"I'm okay," Eddie said quietly.

"His name was Brandt Tinkers, right?" Cassie was determined to pursue this. She was sure Jerry knew something that could help them.

"Yeah. And he was a businessman. That's all I know," Jerry said. "I wasn't here when they brought him in. I don't know where he came from. He was in an accident or something. That's all I know."

We *know* he was in an accident, Cassie thought. *We* killed him.

Again, the scene on Route 12 played through her

mind. The bump. The horrifying bump. The wide-eyed stare of surprise on Tinkers's face. The corpse by the side of the road.

"Really. That's all I- know," Jerry repeated. "And, then, the stiff just disappeared. He was here when you called me, Eddie. Here one minute. Then gone the next."

"Like he walked away," Eddie muttered. "That's what you said, Jerry. You said it was like he walked away."

"Well, maybe I said that," Jerry replied, brushing back his hair again, "but I saw the condition he was in. Believe me, Eddie, he was not ticklish. Not ticklish. There was no way that stiff could get up and walk out of here. Unless — "

"Unless what?" Cassie asked eagerly.

"Unless he's a zombie!" Jerry cried. "The Living Dead!" He whooped with laughter.

"That's not funny," Cassie said quietly.

"Let's go," Eddie urged her. "Let's get out of here."

"You didn't see anyone come in here?" Cassie demanded, ignoring Eddie. "What about Tinkers's family? Don't they want to know what happened to his body? What about the police?"

Jerry shrugged. He burped loudly. "Sorry. Talking about stiffs always makes me hungry."

Neither Cassie nor Eddie smiled.

"You guys sure are serious today. Guess you're upset about Winks, huh?"

"Yeah, we're upset," Cassie said.

"Me, too," Jerry said. "But I don't see what it has to do with the missing stiff."

"I'll show you," Cassie said. She reached into her bag and pulled out the Polaroid snapshot.

"Hey!" Eddie cried in surprise. "You brought that?"

Cassie handed it to Jerry.

Jerry squinted at it, studying it. "That's the stiff!" he cried. "Where'd you get this?"

"It was left for us," Cassie told him. "Someone wants us to think that Tinkers was driving the car that hit Winks."

"We've got to go," Eddie said, jumping to his feet. "I feel really sick."

"I don't get it," Jerry said, staring hard at the snapshot.

"There was a note," Cassie told him. "It said, 'One down, three to go.' "

"Whoa," Jerry said, his face filled with confusion.

Eddie grabbed the photo from him. "Come on, Cassie." He started toward the door.

Cassie saw that Jerry had a very upset look on his face. "Eddie — " he called.

Eddie, halfway across the large room, turned.

"Eddie, I'll call you later," Jerry said. He nodded to Cassie. "See you. Tell Winks I'm pulling for him."

Cassie followed Eddie out of the room and through the long, narrow corridor to the building exit. The sour smell, the smell of death, followed them out into the street.

They didn't say anything to each other until they had walked a couple of blocks and the smell had begun to evaporate. "Jerry sure looked upset," Cassie said thoughtfully.

"I think it's because he saw I was feeling really sick," Eddie said.

"No, I think it was more than that," Cassie replied.

The sun was high in a cloudless sky. The air was crisp and cold. Cassie took a deep breath, then another.

"Sorry I had to get out of there so fast. I just couldn't stay another second," Eddie said as they crossed the street to the bus stop. "I thought I was going to puke my guts out."

"That's okay," Cassie replied. She wasn't thinking about Eddie. She was thinking about Jerry. "I think Jerry got upset when he saw the snapshot because he knows something he's not telling us," she said.

Eddie shrugged. "He said he didn't know anything at all. I really don't think he does."

"When he calls you later, see what you can find out," Cassie instructed.

"Okay," Eddie said. His cheeks were red as usual. But he looked as if he were starting to revive.

* * *

After lunch, Cassie practiced driving with her father. He seemed really nervous, even though she drove slowly and carefully. Sitting beside her in the front passenger seat, he kept slamming his foot down, as if he were applying the brake.

"I think you're going to pass easily tomorrow," he said after she had successfully parallel-parked twice without any trouble.

"You're just desperate to go home," she teased.

He admitted that practicing with her made him a little nervous. Obligingly, she turned the wheel over to him. He dropped her off at the hospital.

The news there was good. Mrs. Winkleman greeted Cassie with happy tears in her eyes. Winks was awake. He was still somewhat groggy. But he was awake. He had several broken ribs, a broken arm, and a sprained knee. Aside from that, he seemed to be fine. He was going to be okay.

"That's wonderful!" Cassie exclaimed, hugging Winks's mother joyfully.

Winks wasn't allowed any visitors yet, so Cassie called her dad to come pick her up. He let her drive home. Cassie couldn't wait to call Scott and Eddie and tell them the good news about their friend.

That night, she tried to push away thoughts of the driver's test so that she could concentrate on her government textbook. It was a little after eleven. Her parents had gone to bed early. She was the only one still up.

She had changed into her warmest, most comfortable nightgown and had just started reading the opening paragraph on the separation of powers when she heard the sound from outside.

A scrabbling sound.

A scraping.

The squeak of a door.

It sounded like the front porch door. She had noticed that squeak the day before when she and her dad spent the day out there sanding.

Curious, Cassie ran to her bedroom window, pushed aside the curtains, and looked down.

"Oh!"

Someone in a dark coat was running across the front yard.

She could only see his back as he disappeared into the shadows of the tall hedges.

Gripped with fear, she stood staring down at the front yard for several seconds after the dark figure had disappeared. Then she reluctantly made her way down the stairs, walking silently so as not to wake her parents.

She hesitated at the front door.

And listened.

She heard a scraping sound. Repeat itself. Again. Again.

Was he out there?

Had he come back?

No. She had seen him run away.

He had definitely been on the porch.

Most likely, he had left something there.

Something frightening? Another ugly photograph? Another threatening note?

She raised her hand to the doorknob. She unlocked the door.

She started to turn the knob — but then stopped.

Should she open the door?

16
Where's Scott?

Cassie clicked on the porch light. Then, holding her breath, she pulled open the heavy wooden front door.

And stared out through the glass of the storm door.

No one there. The porch was empty.

But the scraping sound continued.

Beyond the porch, trees bowed and trembled in a strong, gusting wind. Dead leaves rustled across the yard.

Hesitantly, she pushed open the storm door.

Her legs were shaking, she realized. She still hadn't dared to breathe.

She leaned forward into the rectangle of yellow light.

The scraping sound — she could see now what was causing it.

A large, brown oak leaf was caught in the porch

screen. The wind kept scraping it against the screen.

Cassie finally breathed, exhaling noisily.

A sigh of relief. But the relief lasted only until she saw a large, brown envelope tucked into the porch door.

She had been right.

Whoever had been darting away into the shadows had left an envelope.

Cassie peered out into the darkness, trying to make sure that he hadn't come back, that he wasn't lurking there by the side of the porch, waiting to grab her when she came out for the envelope.

She didn't see anyone.

The leaf scraped against the screen. The wind swirled.

Letting go of the storm door handle, she dashed onto the porch, the cold floor against her bare feet sending a chill up her entire body.

She grabbed the envelope, tugged it out from the porch door, and leapt back into the safety of the house.

Holding the envelope under her arm, she silently closed the front door and carefully locked it. Then she tiptoed up the stairs to her room, shivering, the sound of the rushing wind, the scraping leaf, following her up the stairs.

Shaking from the cold, and from her fright, she climbed into bed, hoping to get warm there, holding the envelope in one hand, tugging the covers up with the other. Then, with a trembling hand, she tore open the envelope.

As she had imagined, it contained another Polaroid photo and another note.

She gasped as she held the snapshot under her bedtable lamp.

There he was again. The corpse. The wide-eyed corpse, posing for the camera.

He was standing on Cassie's front porch. One hand was on the doorknob of the front door.

He was here, Cassie realized.

At my house. Standing on my porch. Standing at the door.

"And then I saw him run away," she said aloud.

So he isn't dead, she realized.

Brandt Tinkers isn't dead. He's alive. And he's trying to terrify us.

No.

He *is* dead.

We saw him. We saw his sunken eyes.

I could smell that he was dead, she told herself.

He was at the morgue. Dead. Dead. Dead.

But then he left the morgue. . . .

This wild, unconnected thinking was leading nowhere. She closed her eyes, counted to ten.

The note. She had forgotten to read the note.

It was on a folded-up sheet of lined notebook paper.

It didn't take long to read. It contained only two words, scrawled in crayoned block letters:

YOU'RE NEXT.

She knew she wasn't thinking clearly. But she had to talk to someone. She was too scared to go to sleep, too scared to sit there shivering under the covers, seeing the corpse standing on her porch, seeing the two scrawled words, seeing the threat again and again.

She couldn't tell her parents.

Then they would have to be told everything, about how Cassie and her friends had taken Eddie's car and gone out driving without any licenses. How they had hit and killed Brandt Tinkers and left him beside the road, desperate not to get into trouble.

Trouble.

Trouble seemed like such a weak word for what was going on.

No, she couldn't tell her parents, even though she really wanted to. It wouldn't be fair to the others.

So whom could she call? Eddie? No. She didn't want to frighten him more. He was already to the breaking point.

Winks? No. Of course not.

She had to call Scott.

She didn't care what time it was. She just had to talk to him.

Scott would calm her down. Scott would understand. Maybe she and Scott could come up with a plan. Maybe they could figure out what was going on.

Her hand was shaking so violently, it took three tries to punch in Scott's number. Sitting up in bed, she listened to the phone ring, gripping the top of the blanket tightly with her free hand.

It rang four times before someone at Scott's house picked it up. Then it took a long while before the voice finally said, "Hello?" in a sleep-fogged voice.

It was Scott's mother.

"I'm sorry to call so late, Mrs. Baldwin," Cassie said in a shrill voice she didn't recognize. "But can I talk to Scott? It's pretty important."

"Who is this? Cassie?" Scott's mother wasn't entirely awake.

"Yes. Could I please talk to him? I'm really sorry."

"But, Cassie, he's asleep. His fever hasn't broken."

"Yes. Please. Please wake him up. I just need to talk to him about . . . something. Please," Cassie begged.

The line was silent for a long time.

All Cassie could hear was her own rapid breathing.

"Well, I'll see if I can wake him," Mrs. Baldwin said finally.

"Oh, thank you."

Cassie heard the phone clank, as if hitting the

floor. Through the phone she heard footsteps, the groan of floorboards, the sound of Mrs. Baldwin going down the hall to wake Scott.

It seemed to take forever.

Cassie sat rigidly in her bed, her back against the hard headboard, her hand still gripping the top of the blanket, the phone receiver pressed tightly to her ear.

Finally, she heard footsteps approaching the phone, then the sound of someone fumbling for the receiver on the other end.

"Cassie — " It was Mrs. Baldwin, sounding wide awake now, and very frightened.

"Cassie, Scott isn't there! He's gone!"

17
Cassie Is Next

Cassie stepped out under a dark, threatening sky.

She shifted her heavy backpack on her shoulders and, bowing her head against the wind, trudged down the driveway and headed toward school.

It had rained during the night. The ground was soft and puddled.

"I should've worn boots," she said aloud, glancing down at her sneakers.

She hopped over a large gray puddle and stepped into the street. A stream of water rolled down the curbside, flowing like a small river into the drain.

It must've rained really hard, she realized. Funny. I didn't hear it.

She always liked to lie in bed and listen to the soft whisper of rain on the roof. It made her feel so warm and protected.

Shifting the backpack again, stepping around a

deep, muddy puddle in the street, she felt unsettled now.

So many troubling thoughts.

So many fears pulling her one way, then another.

She realized she felt weary, even though she had just woken up.

A horn honked behind her.

Cassie let out a startled yelp and leapt to the curb as the North Avondale bus rumbled by. She recognized several kids on the bus. She waved, but they stared back at her, faces distorted in the window glass, and didn't wave back.

It's so cold and windy, she thought, rewrapping the red wool scarf around her neck. I should've taken the bus.

Only two more blocks to walk.

A dog barked from the front stoop of an old red brick house across the street.

The sky grew even darker. Two cars passed, their headlights cutting through the morning darkness.

What day is this? Cassie asked herself. Is it Monday?

Why couldn't she remember?

Such a simple thing. Why couldn't she remember what day it was?

She was still trying to remember when she realized the car was following her.

She turned her head, the backpack straps straining against her chest.

It was a black car. A big black car with heavy chrome all over the front. Its headlights were dark. The windshield was dark. She couldn't see the driver.

It pulled up behind her, then slowed.

Cassie moved to the curb.

The car didn't speed up. Didn't pass her.

Who is it? she wondered, staring hard into the darkened windshield. What do they want?

She started to walk faster.

The car picked up speed.

She started to run.

The car picked up more speed.

Gripped with fear, Cassie tried to utter a cry for help. But no sound came out.

She tried again to scream.

Silence.

She leapt over the curb, her sneakers splashing through tall grass, and onto the sidewalk.

To her horror, the car roared off the road, bumped over the curb, and came after her over the sidewalk.

Help!

She tried again to cry out.

Again, no sound came out of her mouth.

It was closing in on her, going to run her down.

She was going to be mowed down, struck — just like Winks.

YOU'RE NEXT.

The words of the note came back to her.

YOU'RE NEXT.

Help me! Won't somebody help me!

The car was inches behind her. The engine roar seemed to surround her, swallow her up.

Help me!

She tossed off the heavy backpack and kept running.

The car rolled over it, making a loud crunching sound as it closed in on her.

Where is everybody? Won't somebody help me? Cassie wondered.

And then, without thinking about it, she spun around.

And peered through the windshield only a few feet from her face.

And saw the corpse behind the wheel.

"Cassie!" he called, his dark eyes aglow, his voice a dry rush of wind.

"Cassie!" he repeated. "Cassie! Cassie! Cassie!"

The throaty whisper of death.

As he moved to run her over, the dead man repeated her name again and again.

"Cassie! Cassie! Cassie!"

18
Why Would Scott Do It?

"Cassie! Cassie! Cassie!"

Cassie felt hands on her shoulders. Someone was shaking her.

"Cassie! Cassie!"

Cassie blinked, struggled to keep her eyes open.

Her mother hovered over her, gently shaking her by the shoulders. "Cassie — wake up."

"Huh?" She coughed, blinked again. Bright sunlight filtered through the curtains at the window.

"I've been trying to wake you up for hours, but you wouldn't move," her mother said, letting go of her shoulders but not backing away.

Cassie sat up and rubbed her eyes.

"You'll be late for school," her mother said, walking over to the window, pushing the curtains aside, and pulling the window open a crack. Cool air immediately rushed into the room.

"I had the *worst* dream," Cassie told her mother,

finally realizing that walking to school, being chased by the corpse in the car, was all a dream, a horrifying dream.

"I couldn't wake you. It was unbelievable," her mother said, picking up a pair of jeans from the floor, folding them, and putting them over a chairback. "Didn't you sleep well last night?"

"No, not too much," Cassie confessed, swinging her legs around and climbing out of bed. Standing up, she felt as if she weighed a thousand pounds.

She stretched.

"Well, hurry up and get dressed. I'll make you some toast you can eat on the way," Mrs. Martin said, heading to the door. "Hurry. You're really late."

Who cares? Cassie thought glumly, watching her mother leave.

She dropped back down onto the bed and buried her face in her still-warm pillow. She'd been wide awake all night, until about five o'clock when she finally succumbed to sleep.

All the while, she'd been thinking about Scott.

Puzzling about Scott.

Torturing herself about Scott.

She knew it couldn't be Scott who had run Winks down. It couldn't be Scott who was terrifying Eddie and her, threatening them, threatening to run them down, too.

It couldn't be Scott. No way.

But all the evidence pointed to Scott.

Where was he last night when Cassie had called?

He was supposedly sick in bed with a very high fever. But when his mother went to wake him up, he was gone.

Where?

Cassie knew where. He was out putting a frightening photo and note on her porch.

Where did he get the corpse? Why was he using the corpse to scare them? Why had he tried to kill his good friend Winks?

Why did he want to kill her next?

Those questions Cassie couldn't answer.

But she knew why he wasn't in his bed last night.

She had seen him scampering into the hedges after leaving the brown envelope for her.

There were other signs that also pointed to Scott.

The Polaroid pictures. The three of them had teased him about his new Polaroid camera.

And in the first photo, the corpse had been sitting in Scott's car.

And Scott was the only one who hadn't received any frightening phone calls or notes.

It all added up to Scott.

But why?

It made no sense. It couldn't be Scott, she told herself.

Couldn't. Couldn't. Couldn't.

Still not fully awake, still feeling unsettled, flashes of her terrifying dream lingering in her mind, Cassie sat up and reached for the phone.

She hesitated for a second, then took a deep breath and punched in Scott's number.

She had to ask him why he wasn't home in bed in the middle of the night. She had to ask him where he was. She had to know.

She let the phone ring twelve times.

No one answered.

"Cassie, where are you?" her mother called from downstairs.

She replaced the receiver and forced herself to stand up. "I just want to stay in bed," she said to herself in the mirror over the dresser.

But she couldn't. For one thing, she had her driver's test that afternoon.

This was supposed to be an exciting day, she thought miserably, pulling on some clothes without even noticing what she had selected.

A few minutes later, she was half-walking, half-jogging to school, chewing on the slice of buttered toast her mother had handed her as she hurried out the door.

At least I'm not being pursued by a corpse in a big black car, she told herself, looking behind her just to make sure.

She arrived at her locker just as the second homeroom bell rang, and spotted Eddie at his locker across the hall. "Hey, Eddie — wait — " she called.

"We're late," Eddie called to her, slamming his locker, turning the combination on his lock. "See you later!"

"No, wait!" she cried and hurried over to him. "I know who it is, Eddie!"

"Huh?" His cheeks turned bright pink as his mouth dropped in surprise.

"I know!" Cassie declared.

"Eddie, are you coming in? I'm closing the door now." Mr. Murphy, Eddie's homeroom teacher, peered out from the doorway.

Eddie gave Cassie a helpless shrug. "Gotta run. Later — okay?" He started toward his room. "What are you doing after school?"

"Taking my driver's test," Cassie called, disappointed that she didn't get to confide in Eddie, didn't get to tell him about last night.

The door closed behind him.

She stood in the middle of the hall for a while, uncertain of what to do.

It was going to be a long day.

Cassie's driver's test seemed to be over almost before it had begun.

To her surprise, the test was given by a young woman. She made Cassie feel comfortable right away. Cassie drove a few blocks, made a few right and left turns, made a successful U-turn, and parallel-parked between two poles.

"That was easy, wasn't it?" the young examiner said, unbuckling her seat belt and climbing out of the car. "Go see the man in window eleven for your temporary license. Your real license will be mailed in six weeks."

"You mean I *passed?*" Cassie asked, stunned, still sitting behind the wheel.

The examiner laughed. "That's all there is to it. Drive carefully." She hurried to meet her next test-taker.

"Drive carefully," Cassie repeated to herself. What a joke!

For a few minutes, while taking the test, she had managed to shut out all the frightening events of the past few weeks. But now those two words — "Drive Carefully" — had brought it all rushing back to her.

This is a big day in my life, she told herself. I should go out and celebrate tonight.

But she certainly didn't feel like celebrating.

Her parents noticed her lack of enthusiasm at dinner. "Aren't you thrilled about passing your test the first time?" her mother asked.

"Guess we'll never see you anymore," her dad said, only half-joking. And then he added, "I thought you'd be more excited."

Cassie struggled to swallow a piece of chicken. "I — I guess I don't really believe it yet," she replied. It was a lame excuse, she realized, but her parents seemed to buy it.

She hurried up to her room after dinner, intent on calling Scott.

But the moment she started to lift the receiver, the phone rang. "Oh!" she cried, startled, and picked it up, somehow expecting it to be Scott on the other end.

"Hi, Cassie." It was Eddie.

"You scared me," she said. "I was just going to call Scott and — "

"Did you pass it?" he asked eagerly.

"Yes. It was easy," she told him. "I couldn't believe how easy it was."

"You got it? You got your license?"

"Yeah. They give you a temporary card right away," she replied.

"Well, can you take me driving tonight?" he asked.

"Huh? Tonight? Eddie — "

"My mom said if you passed your test, she'd let me borrow the car tonight if you wanted to take me to practice. My test is Friday, see."

"Well, I don't know. . . ." Cassie said reluctantly.

"Please," he begged. "It's my only night to practice before my test."

"I'm really tired," Cassie said truthfully. She'd barely been able to keep her eyes open during dinner.

"Pretty please," Eddie pleaded. "You said you wanted to talk to me, remember? This morning when we were late?"

"Yeah, I guess," Cassie said. She did want to tell Eddie about Scott, and about the photo and note she'd received. "Okay. I'll be right over," she said wearily. "But we'll just drive for a short while, okay?"

"Great! Thanks!" Eddie replied gratefully. "Hurry!" He hung up.

She put down the receiver, then picked it up and punched in Scott's number.

A busy signal.

Well, at least someone was home.

She'd try him again later, she decided, after she discussed everything with Eddie.

It was a clear, cold evening, an orange moon still rising in the navy blue sky. Cassie walked to Eddie's. He lived too nearby to drive there. His parents weren't home. They climbed into the old Chevy, Eddie behind the wheel, and took off.

Eddie seemed more excited than usual, his cheeks blushing, his wiry body tense, hyper. As they drove through town, Cassie described the driver's test to him, step by step.

He agreed that it sounded like a breeze.

He pulled too quickly through a four-way stop. Cassie told him to be more careful.

Before she realized it, they were past town and heading along Route 12, nearly deserted as always.

"Let's not go too far, okay, Eddie? I really am tired tonight. Didn't sleep," Cassie said, glancing at the dashboard clock.

"I talked to Winks," Eddie said. "He called me. Isn't that great?"

"How did he sound?" Cassie asked, very pleased.

"Like Winks," Eddie replied. "He sounded the

same. He's going to be okay. He said he might even get sprung from the hospital next week."

"Oh, that's great news!" Cassie exclaimed. "A little more to the right, Eddie. You're going over the center line."

"Oh. Sorry. I wasn't paying attention," he apologized, turning the wheel. "Tell me what you were going to tell me this morning. You said you know who's scaring us."

"Yeah. I mean, I think I know," Cassie said. "The only problem is, I don't know *why* he's doing it. It doesn't really make any sense."

"Well, why don't you keep a person in suspense?" Eddie said sarcastically, slowing down as an oncoming oil truck roared past.

Cassie took a deep breath and then told Eddie about the night before, about the note and the snapshot, seeing the figure run across her yard, trying to phone Scott, Scott being missing in the middle of the night.

Eddie's face froze in surprise. He kept shaking his head as he drove. "I don't believe it," he muttered. "How could Scott do that to Winks? I mean — "

He started to say something else. But a sudden explosion — like a burst of gunfire — rocked the car.

Cassie screamed.

Eddie hit the brakes as the car careened out of control.

19
Where's the Spare?

The car squealed to a stop on the soft dirt shoulder of the highway and bounced a few times.

Eddie, both hands gripping the wheel, his eyes wide with shock, stared straight ahead through the windshield.

Cassie waited for her heart to stop pounding, then turned to Eddie. "We're okay."

"Yeah," he said, swallowing hard.

"I think you've had a blowout."

He looked very bewildered. "You mean — a tire?"

"Yeah. A flat tire," Cassie said. She pushed open her door. "Let's take a look."

She stepped out into the darkness. She could see immediately that the right rear tire had gone flat.

"Hey, aren't you coming out?" she called. Eddie hadn't moved from behind the wheel. In the dim light from the car ceiling, she could see him staring straight ahead, as if thinking hard, concentrating on something.

"Eddie?"

He spun around, finally hearing her. "Oh. Sorry."

Shaking his head, he climbed out of the car and came around to her side. "Oh, no," he groaned.

"It's just a flat," Cassie said, surprised by how upset he was. "We can fix it real fast. All those tire-changing practices in driver's ed will actually come in handy."

"No," Eddie said softly.

"Huh?" Cassie started around to the driver's side.

Eddie said something from behind the car, but she didn't hear him. She reached under the steering wheel, turned off the ignition, and pulled the key out.

"No," Eddie said, holding his hand up to stop her as she came back around to the trunk.

"Really, Eddie," she said impatiently. "It's just a flat tire. It's not the end of the world."

"We can't fix it," Eddie insisted, his eyes wild.

He's still frightened from the blowout, Cassie thought. It *was* pretty frightening. The first thing I thought was that someone was shooting at us. How awful! Poor Eddie must've been really scared, too.

"Tell you what," she offered. "Help me haul out the spare, and I'll change the tire. Do you have a flashlight in the trunk? You can hold the light on it. It's so dark out here."

"No," Eddie repeated.

"No, what?" Cassie asked, bewildered.

"I don't have a spare," he said.

"You don't?" she cried, surprised. "You must have one. Come on. Let's check."

She put the key in the trunk lock.

"No!" Eddie cried, and lunged toward her. "I don't have a spare, Cassie. Don't open the trunk."

"Eddie — "

"Don't open the trunk!"

He made a desperate grab for the key, but he was too late.

Cassie turned the key in the lock, and the trunk lid popped open.

She peered inside.

Then she raised both hands to her face and started to scream.

20
Just a Joke

Folded neatly in the trunk, its arms and legs tucked in like a laundered shirt, the corpse stared up at Cassie with its dull, lifeless eyes.

Its gray face held a distorted smile. Some stitching on the lips had popped open. A piece of skin on the forehead had peeled back, revealing dark bone.

"No!" She screamed and took a step back.

"I warned you," Eddie said softly.

"Eddie — " She couldn't take her eyes off the corpse, folded so neatly, so carefully in the center of the trunk. "Eddie — it's been *you* all along!"

Eddie had moved behind her and blocked her path. "I'm real sorry," he said, his voice barely a whisper. "I'm real sorry, Cassie."

She whirled around to face him, but the staring dead eyes of the corpse stayed in her mind. "Eddie — I don't understand."

"I'm real sorry," he repeated, his dark eyes staring hard into hers. "I wasn't ready for you. This wasn't supposed to happen yet."

He took a step toward her, his eyes unblinking, as unblinking as the dead man's, his expression tense, studying her face.

"But, why?" Cassie managed to ask. "Why have you been doing this to us?"

A small pickup truck roared by without slowing. There was no other traffic in sight.

A cold wind swirled about them, bending the tall grass in the fields on both sides of the narrow highway.

Cassie was too frightened, too confused, to notice the wind.

"Why, Eddie? What are you doing with this — this corpse?" she asked, not recognizing her shrill, frightened voice.

"It was just a joke," he said softly, his hands stiffly at his sides. "Just a joke. At least it started out that way."

"A joke?" Cassie glanced into the open trunk, then quickly away.

The corpse stared out at her. The dim trunk light made its skin a hideous green.

She felt sick. Her legs were shaking. Her whole body trembled.

"Everyone hates me," Eddie said, without any emotion at all, his eyes staring straight ahead at her, his face a blank. "Everyone hates me. No one cares. No one."

"That's not true — " she interrupted.

But he raised a hand to silence her.

"It *is* true," he insisted, raising his voice to a shout. "Why else would they play all the jokes on me? Winks and everyone else. Always trying to make me look like a fool, always trying to scare me to death."

"But, Eddie — "

"I *know* they all call me Scaredy Katz," he continued heatedly, balling and unballing his fists. "I know they all laugh at me, think I'm a chicken. Winks and Scott — and you, too, Cassie."

"Eddie, people only play jokes on people they *like*," Cassie said. She knew it was lame, but the hatred on Eddie's face, the uncontrolled anger, was really terrifying her.

"That's a stupid lie!" Eddie screamed. "Everyone makes fun of me. Everyone makes fun of Scaredy Katz. Everyone tries to frighten me, tries to make me feel like I'm some kind of poor, timid freak."

"Eddie — "

Cassie didn't know what to say.

In a way, Eddie was right. They had all been cruel to him. But no one realized how deeply he had felt the pain from their jokes.

They were just jokes, after all.

"So I decided to show *you* what it's like to be scared. Really scared," Eddie said, his face filled with menace now as he took a step toward Cassie. "I worked it all out myself. My own little practical joke. First, I borrowed the corpse from Jerry. Then — "

Cassie gasped. "Wait a minute, Eddie," she cried, raising both hands to her face. "Wait a minute. Do you mean that we didn't kill this guy? We didn't hit him that night in your car?"

A pleased grin spread slowly across Eddie's face.

"You were all so stupid," he said scornfully. "We didn't kill him. He'd been dead for days. He was so stiff, he stood up by himself."

21
Run!

Eddie shook his head, grinning at her.

Cassie suddenly felt weak.

All that guilt, she thought. All those nightmares.

We all felt so terrible. Like criminals.

And Tinkers had already been dead.

He'd been dead for days.

"Jerry helped you do this?" Cassie cried, her voice revealing her fear, her confusion.

"He was up on the underpass," Eddie said, still grinning, a grin of triumph. "Jerry stood the corpse in the road when he saw my car coming."

"But — but who *is* he?" she demanded, glancing to the open car trunk.

"Some homeless guy," Eddie replied, shrugging his narrow shoulders. "No one claimed him. So Jerry let me borrow him."

"So that you could terrify us? So that you could

mow Winks down? So that you could *kill* us?"

The grin faded from Eddie's face. "I wanted you to know what it's like to be afraid, really afraid."

"But, Eddie — "

"I wanted you to think that the corpse was coming after you, that it had come back to life, that it wanted to take its revenge. But you were too smart for that. You didn't believe it was the corpse."

He closed his eyes. He let out a long cry, a cry of anger mixed with sadness. "So I decided to do more than frighten you. I decided to pay you back. For all the jokes. For all the laughter. For all the times you frightened me and made me feel like a cowardly baby!"

He was shouting now, his dark eyes blazing, his face quivering, out of control as his fury escaped.

"I got Winks. Scaredy Katz got Winks. I showed him. Now, it's your turn, Cassie!"

"No!" she cried, her mind spinning desperately, trying to think of something to say to him, something to calm him.

But it was too late.

He had reached into the trunk and pulled out a tire iron. "Your turn, Cassie," he said, raising it menacingly over his head, moving toward her quickly. "Your turn!"

"Eddie — no!" she screamed, raising her hands in front of her as if they could protect her. "No!"

He stopped, holding the tire iron high. "Don't

worry. I'm going to give you a chance." He gestured with the tire iron, swinging it wildly. "Go on. Get going. Run!"

"Oh!" Cassie spun around, trying to focus her eyes on the dark countryside. There was nowhere to run. Nowhere to hide. Stretching on both sides of the deserted highway was nothing but flat, open grassland.

"Run!" Eddie screamed, his voice raw and threatening behind her. "Run!"

Cassie started to run down the highway, bending low into the swirling wind.

"Run! Run!"

She could still hear Eddie screaming.

And then the screaming stopped. And the only sound was the rapid *thud* of her sneakers against the pavement.

She heard the roar of the car engine.

Spinning around, the white light of the headlights caught her, trapped her, blinded her for a moment. She stood paralyzed, like a frightened rabbit.

The lights grew brighter.

The car roared forward.

He's going to run me down, she realized.

22

Smashup

The lights grew brighter, blindingly bright.

Cassie tried to run, but it was too late.

Even with its flat tire, the car was coming too fast. The roar of its engine drowned out the *flap flap flap* of the empty rear tire, drowned out all of Cassie's thoughts, seemed to encircle her, pull her in.

She cried out as she heard the crash.

I'm dead, she thought.

I'm hit.

He's killed me.

She waited for the pain, the overwhelming pain, waited for the darkness to fall over her.

But the crash continued behind her.

The crush of metal against metal.

The crunch and tinkle of shattering glass.

The squeal of tires as they skidded over the pavement.

I'm not hit, she realized.

I'm okay!

She turned to see that another car had barreled into the side of Eddie's Chevy. Another car had collided with the old Chevy, pushed it off the road onto the soft shoulder.

A silver Volvo.

Scott's car.

The driver's door opened, and Scott climbed out. "Cassie?"

She ran to him. "Scott! Scott! I'm here!" She threw herself into Scott's arms, pressing her face against his down coat. "It was Eddie," she cried. "Eddie. He wanted to kill us."

"I know," Scott said softly.

It took Cassie a while to realize that someone else had climbed out of Scott's car. It was Jerry. He ran to the Chevy and dragged Eddie out of the car.

"Jerry — what are *you* doing here?" Eddie cried, his face filled with confusion. "Why'd you wreck my car?"

Jerry pulled Eddie roughly over to Cassie and Scott. The four of them stood spotlighted in the Volvo's headlights. Jerry held Eddie tightly by the shoulders.

"It was supposed to be a joke, Eddie," Jerry cried angrily. "You said it was going to be a joke. You never said anything about running people down, hurting people."

"It *was* a joke," Eddie said, his dark eyes wild, darting from one of them to the other. "It was a big joke."

"People got hurt, Eddie," Jerry said, holding on to his cousin tightly. "Winks is your friend. You nearly killed him."

"No one is my friend," Eddie said bitterly.

"How did you find us?" Cassie asked Scott, still leaning against him, still feeling as if she needed his protection. "How did you know where we were?"

"I took a guess," Scott replied. "Jerry called me. He said he was real worried about Eddie."

"Yeah," Jerry interrupted, looking at Eddie. "When I saw those Polaroids yesterday when you came to the morgue, I knew something was wrong. I knew Eddie was up to something bad. I've been trying to reach him ever since."

"Eddie's mom told us you took him driving," Scott said, his arm around her, warming her, calming her. "So I just figured we'd find you here on Route 12."

"I'm so glad," Cassie said, sighing.

But then she suddenly remembered something. She pulled away from Scott and eyed him coldly. "Scott, I have to ask you something."

"Huh?"

"Where were you last night? In the middle of the night? I called you. Your mom went to look for you, and you were gone. I was so frightened, I started to think — "

Scott put a warm hand over her mouth to cut her off. "I was sleepwalking," he told her. "Sometimes I do that when I have a high fever. It's really kind of scary. Mom found me walking behind the garage. She led me back to my room."

"Sleepwalking?" Cassie cried.

"I don't remember it at all," Scott said.

"I tried to call you this morning — " Cassie started.

"Mom took me to the doctor first thing," Scott told her. "But he doesn't have a cure for sleep-walking. It's happened to me a few times before. It's so scary. Luckily, my fever is down."

"You're weird," Jerry told Scott.

"Let me go," Eddie insisted, struggling to break away from his cousin.

"Take it easy," Jerry insisted. "We're going to get you the help you need, Eddie."

"Help? I don't need help!" Eddie cried.

"We'll have to take my car," Scott said, walking toward the two cars. "Eddie's car is pretty banged up."

"And it has a flat tire," Cassie told them. "That's how I discovered the corpse. I opened the trunk and — "

"The corpse? It's here?" Jerry asked, surprised.

"In Eddie's trunk," Cassie said, picturing the torn forehead, the dull, sunken eyes.

"Well, let's get it out so I can return it," Jerry said, still holding on to Eddie, but moving quickly toward Eddie's car. "Okay if we put it in your trunk, Scott?"

"I guess," Scott said reluctantly, a sick look on his face.

Jerry pulled open the Chevy's trunk, and they all peered inside.

The corpse was gone.

23
No More Jokes

Two weeks later, Cassie, Scott, and Jerry were gathered at Winks's house. Winks was still confined to the house. They were doing their best to entertain him and keep him from going stir-crazy.

"And no one ever found the corpse?" Winks asked, raising the cast on his arm so that he could scratch his side with his good hand.

"No." Cassie shook her head.

"Eddie kept insisting it was alive, really alive," Scott said. And then he added, "Poor guy."

"He's getting treatment from good doctors," Jerry said, slouching down on the leather armchair.

"Well, a corpse can't just get up and walk away, can it?" Winks asked, puzzling over this story.

"This one did," Jerry said, shaking his head. "I've handled a lot of corpses. I've had some snorers and some groaners, but this is the first walker."

"Yuck," Cassie said, making a face. "Can't we talk about something else?"

"Hey, Jerry," Winks said, pushing himself up with the cast on his arm, "will you lend me another eyeball when I go back to school?"

"No way, man," Jerry said, holding up his hands. "No more jokes for me. I've learned my lesson. No more jokes" — and then he added slyly — "if I can help it."

Everyone laughed.

"Hey, I've got to get some sleep," Scott said, glancing at his watch. "I've got my driver's test tomorrow." He stood up. "When's your test, Winks?"

"Forget it," Winks said glumly. "From now on, I'm taking the bus."

They all headed to the front door, Winks walking slowly but deliberately, limping only slightly. He pulled open the door for them.

And then they all screamed in horror.

The corpse was standing in the doorway, his face pressed against the storm door. His sunken eyes stared blindly into the house. The skin flap on his forehead had pulled further open, revealing more skull.

"No!" Cassie cried. "This is impossible!"

"How did he find us?" Winks cried.

Jerry's face filled with amusement. "One last joke, guys!" he exclaimed. "Sorry." He couldn't contain his laughter, which burst out as he surveyed their reactions.

"I found it on the side of the road that night," he explained. "In the tall grass. Eddie must have tossed it out of the trunk before he came after you, Cassie."

"So you went back and got it?" Cassie demanded.

Jerry nodded. "I've been saving it for just the right moment," he declared.

"Well, this wasn't it!" Cassie said.

"Let's get him!" Scott cried.

Jerry pushed open the storm door, toppling the well-traveled corpse, and started to run full speed down the drive, with Cassie and Scott in close pursuit.

Winks watched them chase Jerry down the block.

Then he stepped out onto the stoop and propped the corpse back up in front of the door.

"Hey, Mom! Dad!" he called, stepping back into the house. "There's someone at the door who wants to see you!"

About the Author

R.L. STINE is the author of more than eighty books of humor, adventure, and mystery for young readers. He has written more than twenty thrillers such as this one.

In addition to his publishing work, he is head writer of the children's TV show *Eureeka's Castle*, seen on Nickelodeon.

He lives in New York City with his wife, Jane, and their son, Matt.

THRILLERS

Nobody Scares 'Em Like R.L. Stine

point® **THRILLERS**

R.L. Stine

- ☐ MC44236-8 The Baby-sitter — $3.50
- ☐ MC44332-1 The Baby-sitter II — $3.50
- ☐ MC45386-6 Beach House — $3.25
- ☐ MC43278-8 Beach Party — $3.50
- ☐ MC43125-0 Blind Date — $3.50
- ☐ MC43279-6 The Boyfriend — $3.50
- ☐ MC44333-X The Girlfriend — $3.50
- ☐ MC45385-8 Hit and Run — $3.25
- ☐ MC46100-1 The Hitchhiker — $3.50
- ☐ MC43280-X The Snowman — $3.50
- ☐ MC43139-0 Twisted — $3.50

Caroline B. Cooney

- ☐ MC44316-X The Cheerleader — $3.25
- ☐ MC41641-3 The Fire — $3.25
- ☐ MC43806-9 The Fog — $3.25
- ☐ MC45681-4 Freeze Tag — $3.25
- ☐ MC45402-1 The Perfume — $3.25
- ☐ MC44884-6 The Return of the Vampire — $2.95
- ☐ MC41640-5 The Snow — $3.25
- ☐ MC45682-2 The Vampire's Promise — $3.50

Diane Hoh

- ☐ MC44330-5 The Accident — $3.25
- ☐ MC45401-3 The Fever — $3.25
- ☐ MC43050-5 Funhouse — $3.25
- ☐ MC44904-4 The Invitation — $3.50
- ☐ MC45640-7 The Train (9/92) — $3.25

Sinclair Smith

- ☐ MC45063-8 The Waitress — $2.95

Christopher Pike

- ☐ MC43014-9 Slumber Party — $3.50
- ☐ MC44256-2 Weekend — $3.50

A. Bates

- ☐ MC45829-9 The Dead Game — $3.25
- ☐ MC43291-5 Final Exam — $3.25
- ☐ MC44582-0 Mother's Helper — $3.50
- ☐ MC44238-4 Party Line — $3.25

D.E. Athkins

- ☐ MC45246-0 Mirror, Mirror — $3.25
- ☐ MC45349-1 The Ripper — $3.25
- ☐ MC44941-9 Sister Dearest — $2.95

Carol Ellis

- ☐ MC44768-8 My Secret Admirer — $3.25
- ☐ MC46044-7 The Stepdaughter — $3.25
- ☐ MC44916-8 The Window — $2.95

Richie Tankersley Cusick

- ☐ MC43115-3 April Fools — $3.25
- ☐ MC43203-6 The Lifeguard — $3.25
- ☐ MC43114-5 Teacher's Pet — $3.25
- ☐ MC44235-X Trick or Treat — $3.25

Lael Littke

- ☐ MC44237-6 Prom Dress — $3.25

Edited by T. Pines

- ☐ MC45256-8 Thirteen — $3.50

point ®

Other books you will enjoy, about real kids like you!